Now what? Abigail has a lifetime ahead of her. She is raising three children. One lady, and two lords. She is up to the task, but will she have to do it alone?

With her newfound freedom in Australia, she decides to build an estate for herself and her family. Lord Worthington, her oldest son, will inherit his father's estates in England. Her second son, Lord Brentford, will inherit the estate she is building. Her daughter may find an eminently suitable man here, or perhaps she may prefer to go back to England, where society understands nobility, men are plentiful, and she can easily find someone among her peers.

Abigail's choices though, are limited, because the men who would advise her feel compelled to protect the delicate woman they believe her to be. Her determination, her decisions, and her money are her own, and she refuses to allow a man—any man—to keep her from making her dreams a reality.

But as she chips away at her mental lists to realize those dreams, someone, somewhere, has decided the Dowager Countess of Worthington, Lady Abigail, must die.

A K'Anne Meinel novel

Also by K'Anne Meinel:

Novels in Paperback:

SHIPS *CompanionSHIP, FriendSHIP, RelationSHIP*
Long Distance Romance
Children of Another Mother
Erotica
The Claim
Bikini's Are Dangerous
The Complete Series
Germanic
Malice Masterpieces 1
The First Five Books
Represented
Timed Romance
Malice Masterpieces 2
Books Six through Ten
The Journey Home
Out at the Inn
Shorts
Anthology Volume 1
Lawyered
Malice Masterpieces 3
Books Eleven through Fifteen
Blown Away
Blown Away
The Alternate Cover
Small Town Angel
Pirated Love
Doctored
Veil of Silence
Malice Masterpieces 4
Books Sixteen through Twenty
The Outsider
Pirated Heart
Recombinant Love
Survivors
Inn the Dog House
Flight
An Island Between Us
Malice Masterpieces 5
Books Twenty-One through Twenty-Five
Malice Masterpieces 6
Books Twenty-Six through Thirty
Beauty and the Beast
Home ~ The First Nillionaires Club

Vetted Series:

Vetted
Cavalcade (Prequel)
Pioneering (Prequel)
Vetted Further
Vetted Again

Novellas in Paperback:

Sapphic Surfer
Sapphic Cowgirl
Sapphic Cowboi
Sayyida
The Northwood Lodge

The Malice Series:

Mysterious Malice (Book 1)
Meticulous Malice (Book 2)
Mistaken Malice (Book 3)
Malicious Malice (Book 4)
Masterful Malice (Book 5)
Matrimonial Malice (Book 6)
Mourning Malice (Book 7)
Murderous Malice (Book 8)
Mental Malice (Book 9)
Menacing Malice (Book 10)
Minor Malice (Book 11)
Morally Malice (Book 12)
Morose Malice (Book 13)
Melancholy Malice (Book 14)
Mad Malice (Book 15)
Macabre Malice (Book 16)
Marinating Malice (Book 17)
Macerating Malice (Book 18)
Minacious Malice (Book 19)
Meddlesome Malice (Book 20)
Meandering Malice (Book 21)
Maniacal Malice (Book 22)
Monitoring Malice (Book 23)
Marked Malice (Book 24)
Mandating Malice (Book 25)
Methodical Malice (Book 26)
Malevolent Malice (Book 27)
Militarial Malice (Book 28)
Machiavellian Malice (Book 29)
Malefic Malice (Book 30)
Manipulative Malice (Book 31)
Macular Malice (Book 32)

All Novels and Novellas in paperback are also available as e-books.

Novellas in Paperback Continued:

Religious Experience
Lied
The Rockhound Prequel
The Rockhound

A Woman Down Under Series:

Shanghaied (Prequel)
Outback Born
Outback Bred
Outback Heritage
Outback Native
Outback Splendor
Outback Yearnings (Prequel)
Outback Escape
Outback Future
Outback Senora
Outback Lady

Pocket Paperbacks:

Mysterious Malice (Book 1)
Sapphic Surfer
Sapphic Cowgirl
Meticulous Malice (Book 2)
Mistaken Malice (Book 3)
Malicious Malice (Book 4)
Masterful Malice (Book 5)
Matrimonial Malice (Book 6)
Mourning Malice (Book 7)
Murderous Malice (Book 8)
Mental Malice (Book 9)
Menacing Malice (Book 10)
Minor Malice (Book 11)
Morally Malice (Book 12)
Morose Malice (Book 13)
Melancholy Malice (Book 14)
Mad Malice (Book 15)
Macabre Malice (Book 16)
Marinating Malice (Book 17)

In E-Book Format:

Short Stories

Fantasy
Wet & Wet Again
Family Night
Quickie ~ Against the Car
Quickie ~ Against the Wall
Quickie ~ Over the Couch
Mile High Club
Quickie ~ Under the Pier
Heel or Heal
Kiss
Family Night 2
Beach Dreams
Internet Dreamers
Snoggered
On the Parkway
Stable Affair
Kept
Stolen
Agitated
Love of my LIFE
Quickie in an Elevator,
GOING DOWN?
Into the Garden
The Book Case
The Other Women
Menage a WHAT?
The Wicked Stepdaughter
The Gamble

LARGE Print Novels

SHIPS CompanionSHIP, FriendSHIP,
RelationSHIP
Erotica Volume 1
Long Distance Romance
Children of Another Mother
Bikini's Are Dangerous
The Complete Series
Malice Masterpieces
The First Five Books
To Love a Shooting Star
The Claim
Represented
Timed Romance

K'ANNE MEINEL

OUTBACK LADY

Published by Shadoe Publishing

ISBN-13: 978-1-959436-21-8

K'Anne Meinel is available for comments at KAnneMeinel@aim.com as well as on Facebook, Google +, or her blog @ http://kannemeinel.wordpress.com/ or on Twitter @ kannemeinelaim.com, or on her website @ www.kannemeinel.com if you would like to follow her to find out about stories and book's releases.

www.shadoepublishing.com

ShadoePublishing@gmail.com

Shadoe Publishing is a United States of America company

Cover by: K'Anne Meinel

OUTBACK LADY

CHAPTER ONE

Abigail gazed at the cobblestone streets that looked so much like those back in England. The smell of the ocean was strong off the bay. But the different tang in the air told her she was not back in her home country.

Eucalyptus trees were one of a million strange things she had never seen before moving to Australia. She loved to hear the native Australians say the name with their thick accents, although most referred to the plants as gum trees. She had also been told there were some eight hundred different species, native to Australia. Some were even rainbow in color, and the trunks peeled back their own bark.

Even more fascinating were the various birds she saw in their branches. There seemed to be brightly colored birds in every brilliant full spectrum of the rainbow. They were incredible, nothing like

common sparrows, tits, or blackbirds back in England. They were loud, numerous, and entertaining to watch, sometimes they acted almost human. Their intelligence showed in everything they did, which was absolutely fascinating.

Parramatta Road went out past the brickyard and market. As she watched the farmers at the market discuss the merits of sheep, cattle, pigs, and horses, Abigail recalled her forays into the market before she went to the Outback, remembering the excitement of bargaining with the vendors, handling her own money, and buying some of the freshest fruits and vegetables for their table. She would never have done something like that back in England; it wouldn't have been allowed. She turned her fine horse, her escorts on either side turning with her as she headed for the rented house.

It was good to be back in Sydney from her long sojourn into the Outback. Seeing Melissa again had been nice but surprising, enlightening even. She had thought to get her back, her first love, but she realized they had both grown older, and apart, with the passage of time. Melissa, now Mel, was content in her inland kingdom with her wife and children. Abigail supposed she had grown up too.

Watching the two women make a life for themselves in this odd land down under, she couldn't come between them. Their love was real, it was honest, and while not pure in some people's eyes, it worked for those two individuals. She was glad she had done nothing to tear it apart. Now it was time for her to make a life for herself and her three children.

"Mama," Agatha said in a small voice from astride her little pony, "will we be going back?" Her head jerked to point down Parramatta Road.

"Back where, my darling girl?"

"To England?" the little girl asked. She barely remembered the passage they had taken over a year ago.

"No, my dear. There is nothing there for me, for us, anymore. We will bring things here for us and make a life here," she said, gesturing to the odd lands, birds, and even the animals about them, it was quite unlike anything back in England. "We will search for lands of our own here in Australia and build a home and a life here."

Agatha frowned, trying to understand all that. "What about Tante Alinta and Onkel Mel?" she asked, confused. They were, indeed, two of the most important adults in their lives.

Abigail smiled at the German monikers her child had given her friends, a touch of her deceased husband's heritage, and her own need to respect her friends. She couldn't have her children calling adults by their first names, after all. "Ah, they are in the far Outback. We won't be going that far," she assured her, looking down the busy street and guiding her mount through the throng of people.

She thought about the foolish journey she had made with her children into the Outback to see Mel and how arduous it had been. She hadn't understood how dangerous it would be, despite being warned, and how easily this land could have taken all their lives. She also hadn't realized how large this country was or how far she would have to go to get to Mel's enormous Outback station. She looked about the more settled area where they were riding and thought about the people that inhabited this area of the country. While she appreciated the settlement, she knew she wanted something a little more remote, something less populated than Sydney and some of the surrounding villages. She wanted rolling hills, land, and a place to keep her horses

and to allow her children to grow big and strong. She recalled the land beyond the Nepean River and the lack of settlements there.

Her guards moved up slightly, a couple of them calling to the crowds on the road, "Make way there, make way."

Lady Agatha looked up from her pony. "Will Auggie and Mel come with us?"

"Of course," she answered, making certain her Thoroughbred didn't outpace the pony too much. The pony was game, though, and would frequently jog to match its stride, keeping the young lady on her toes to hold the pony in check.

"Do they have to?"

Her daughter's plaintive tone had Lady Abigail smiling. Her brothers could be little monsters, but they adored their older sister. "Yes, they do," she assured the little girl. "Someday, you will appreciate your brothers," she promised. Or at least Abigail hoped she would. Abigail wanted her sons to be much better brothers than her own brothers had proven to be. She wanted her children to share a camaraderie that had been missing for her and her brothers, a love that could never be questioned. "They will be your most loyal admirers."

"Admirers?" the girl asked, frowning again as she tried to understand. She was proving to be an adept pupil, having learned to control her pony well. Abigail was proud of her progress and wondered when she would have to introduce the young girl to a horse of her own and not merely a pony. Regardless, it would be a long time before she would trust the girl with a Thoroughbred, such as the one she was riding.

"That's right," she told her assuredly. "They will defend and protect you as only brothers can." Her own brothers hadn't defended

her or protected her. The oldest, Robert, wasn't willing to help her in the least. Instead, he had been willing to help himself to her own inheritance from her now deceased husband. He'd been influenced by their father, whose greedy fingers couldn't wait to get his hands on Abigail's inheritance, and Abigail had escaped England with her sons in her belly and a daughter whom she barely knew on her lap. She enjoyed her daughter now; she was becoming a little someone she loved talking with.

The four guards kept themselves to each corner of the ladies' ride, making a kind of box, where all who passed had to give way to the ladies and their armed escort. The prisoners, many transported from England, with their ugly yellow convict suits, the villagers, and the farmers all stared at the lady adorned in the finest of clothing, riding astride a valuable horse instead of side-saddle. Abigail didn't care; her skirts were split so she could more easily hold on to the spirited horse. Only recently had she begun riding about, making herself known since she had returned to the Sydney area.

As they made their way back to their rented house and up the drive, boys ran from the stables behind the house to take the bridles and help the ladies down from their mounts. Abigail, an experienced horsewoman needed no help, but her daughter took advantage and was thrilled when they twirled her about, shouting, "Weee!" with absolute glee.

"Come, my darling." Countess Abigail Worthington held out her hand to her daughter, who took it happily, skipping as they walked up onto the porch.

"My lady," a footman said, looking down as he bowed. "I've mailed all your letters and picked up the mail from the post office." He held out the packet.

"More?" she asked, surprised. It had taken her a week to go through all that had been waiting for her when she returned from Mel Lawrence's station. Months of correspondence had been awaiting her return. The return packet of letters she had penned, had been quite substantial too. Her hands had cramped from all the writing she had to pen, taking her time not to hurry or to allow her handwriting to suffer. It wouldn't do for the Countess of Worthington to have sloppy penmanship. She had answered queries from her managers and solicitor, and she had sent out many of her own with instructions, questions, and directions. It had been obvious that they were concerned when she had disappeared into the Outback, despite her letters to them. Many letters had crossed in the mail because they had to travel around the world. She only hoped her new letters would reassure them.

"Aye, m'lady," he told her, pulling at his forelock

"Thank you," she said as she took the packet. She tucked it under her arm and held Lady Agatha's hand as they walked into the house.

"Breakfast, m'lady?" Mrs. Harris asked, pleased to have her there to cook for. She hadn't liked being left behind with the other servants, but not everyone could go into the Outback. From hearing the stories from the guards and maids, she was glad not to have gone on that long and dangerous journey. The maids had told horrific tales of the things they had had to do without, describing the dust, bugs, strange animals, and long trek they endured. They had been gone a long time. Whatever had happened, all of those men and women were changed forever. It appeared that the countess was too.

"Has Leesa fed the boys?" Lady Abigail asked as she stopped in a room they had set aside with a wash basin, she put down the packet to wash her hands and face, so she could wash her daughter's hands and face too and glanced to the screen they set in a corner to hide the commode.

"Aye," Mrs. Harris told her. "They ate in me kitchen not a half an hour ago."

"Good," she said, acknowledging the information. "I'll want to speak to some of the men after breakfast. I'll want some stable boys who know the lay of the land."

"Mr. Clarence can choose what boys you need," she told her, recommending the coachman who had come with them from England.

She nodded, finishing up and picking up her packet.

"Mama, can I have toast and eggs?" Agatha asked, looking at the long table in the dining room that was set for the two of them.

"You can, my darling," her mother agreed, helping her get into her chair and to dish up her plate from the sideboard where the dishes were laid out. Two of the servers exchanged looks, not used to the independence of this lady who would do their jobs.

Abigail served herself, choosing eggs, toast, bacon, and some delicious fruit. She wasn't certain what the different fruits were that were available here in Australia, but Mrs. Harris had been adding them to their diet, assured by the vendors at the market, where she tried them herself before serving them to the household. Abigail was enjoying the different flavors because she had tried some previously when they'd first arrived and she'd bought some of them herself. She grinned, thinking back to those escapades. Many were unavailable in the Outback, but then, they had other odd dishes and fruits.

Abigail went through the packet as she ate, talking to Agatha, who had a delightful take on what they had seen that morning on their ride. The trees along the way were full of birds and other animals, all unusual to them. They were grateful when one of the guards, a villager, or someone shared the animal names and a few things about them.

At the end of her meal, Mrs. Fredericks, the boys' former nursemaid, now their governess, towed both boys in to say good morning to their mother. She left them with their more than capable mother. Abigail put down her mail and devoted time to the growing boys, who also made a beeline for their older sister. Seeing the young girl's annoyance, she suggested that Agatha seek out Bonnie, another nursemaid also made a governess, she had brought with her from England. "If you can't find Bonnie, look for Mrs. Fredericks," she advised the little girl as she ran off. She'd kept on the former wet-nurse as an additional governess to her children, the servant's own son, Joseph allowed to join in with the young lords and lady as a companion to them. With three young children, she wanted them well looked after. Glancing at the men-at-arms disguised as footman at her front door, she mentally added, and protected.

"And how are you, my fine young gentlemen?" she asked her sons, who had tall tales to tell her, and she listened earnestly, as though it were of great importance.

Abigail was devoted to her sons. They were twins. Augustus, named for her deceased husband, was the Earl of Worthington. She had named her second-born son Melbourne Robert, after the famous Australian earl. She had purchased the Earldom of Brentford for him. Auggie and Mel, as she called them, were becoming a handful and she

was glad she'd had the foresight to keep on their nursemaids, make them governesses, and keep valuable and trained servants in this foreign land

After a considerable amount of time had passed and she had given the boys her undivided attention, she noticed the maids clearing the table. She passed the boys off to Mrs. Fredericks, who she knew was nervous about her position here in the household now that her wet-nurse duties were no longer necessary to the young earls. She had thought to train her to be the housekeeper, as she noted Mrs. Harris was becoming more and more busy in the kitchen and couldn't do both. Thinking of that, she halted the woman from leaving.

"Mrs. Fredericks?" she asked the woman who was gathering the boys and the toys they had in their fat little fingers.

"Yes, my lady?" she asked as she made certain the boys didn't leave anything behind.

"I would like you to start training to becoming my housekeeper. Do you think you are up to that position?"

Surprised, the woman blinked. Recovering herself, she nodded most heartily. "Yes, ma'am, I do believe I am."

"Good, start with doing the little things and anything you may need to learn from the other servants and what you've observed in other households. We'll discuss it more as you begin to take over the duties, and perhaps by the time I have a regular house," she gestured at the rental they were living in, "you'll officially be the housekeeper, with a corresponding pay?"

Giving her ladyship a curtsy, the older woman beamed. "Yes, my lady." She gathered the boys once more by the hand and then added a heartfelt, "Thank you."

Content with that duty taken care of, Abigail looked to gathering her papers.

"Ma'am?" a head poked around the corner of the dining room as she rose with her packet of letters.

"Clarence!" she said delightedly, pleased to see her coachman. "Come with me," she said, indicating the way to the library, where she kept her office. It hadn't been used very much because she'd been gone most of the year to visit Mel Lawrence. When she had sat down at the desk and indicated that the coachman could sit down across from her, she began, "I am looking for a man by the name of Shamus O'Grady. He is an Irishman and a builder, and I would like to hire him if he can be found. He built my friends' homes in the Outback," she gestured to the far-off hills beyond Sydney, "and I'd like to talk to him about building me a home here in Australia."

"Then we are definitely staying, ma'am?"

"We are," she confirmed, knowing that the servants must have speculated since she had returned from the Outback, but she was planning on making this huge island her home. Maybe not with Mel, as she had originally thought, but she would build a home here. Someday her second son, Lord Brentford would inherit it from her. Her oldest would inherit the estates back in England that she had saved for him and there would be nothing for her second son that she didn't provide for him. She'd out-maneuvered her father who would have taken it all for himself and gambled away every last bit of it. Her mind had thought it out on the long journey she had made from the Outback, and she knew her destiny was here in Australia. She wondered, would *she* find happiness? Would she, like Mel, find a mate?

"I'd also like to send a man to Mr. Hanneman to renew the rental on this house," she continued, writing a quick note on her stationary. "I should probably see Mr. Saunders," she murmured as she wrote.

"Mr. Hanneman will be relieved to hear from you, m'lady," he assured her. "He was most diligent on checking on the house while you were gone."

She glanced up. "Diligent?"

"I don't think he thought you would come back. He was concerned about getting paid."

She had instructed her solicitor, Mr. Saunders to make the payments on the house, and she glanced around the room, wondering what the property manager was about. "Did Mr. Saunders come around?" she asked casually.

"Aye, once or twice, but not nearly as often as Mr. Hanneman."

She thought about that for a moment before finishing up her note. She lit a candle, waited for the wax to drip on the edge of the note, and pressed her ring into the hot wax to seal it. After she blew out the candle, she addressed it as Clarence waited patiently.

She'd written to her solicitor here in Australia, here in Sydney, upon her return. She made sure to write to Mel—telling of her safe arrival back in civilization. Those had gone out, along with many others, in a large packet. Many of them had gone overseas. One went to Sir Boardman, who handled her estates in England. She'd also written to Mr. Cherwin, the manager of her mills; to Mr. Elmswood, the manager of her breeding farms; and to others she had business with. Glancing through the new packet, she guessed that some of the questions and answers she had sent would pass in the mail and laughed at this occurrence, but it couldn't be helped. Sometimes, the same letter was

sent twice, at least a week apart, in case the first got lost on the way. It was a common enough procedure, something she herself had done on many an occasion.

"Here you go," she said, handing him the missive. "Everything okay with the horses?"

"Aye, everything is fine, m'lady," he assured her. He liked that she had inspected those few horses she had brought with her from England. He took good care of them, her coach, her carriage, and even the lads she'd had him bring. They'd all had a good time of it while she was traveling into the interior, with not much to do, but now that she was back, he was eager to prove that her trust wasn't misplaced.

She dismissed him, smiling as she looked about the house. It didn't need her, and she was restless, anxious to get started on her plans. She was ever so pleased when she sat on the porch, enjoying the beautiful Sydney weather and the passersby she could see down her long drive on the street. She saw a coach turn into the drive and she was there to greet Mr. Saunders as he was let out of his hired coach.

"Lady Worthington," he said by way of greeting, sweeping the top hat from his head, bowing slightly, and then, looking up quickly, he added, "er … Countess."

"It's okay, Mr. Saunders," she said, smiling. "You may call me either. Both are not necessary. Although, technically I am the Dowager Countess of Worthington," she added, thoughtfully, "and my daughter is Lady Worthington until Auggie marries."

He shook his head as he climbed the steps to her porch. The various titles and ways of the British aristocracy were a far cry from Sydney and it's simpler social structure. Although other ladies had moved to

Australia before, they were still rare and cause for people to gossip and stare.

"I received your letter …" he began, trying to get right down to business.

"Please, sit down." She gestured to the other chair, and seeing Mrs. Harris, she ordered, "Bring us something cool to drink?" At the cook's nod she turned back to her guest.

"I thank you for that," he said, using his handkerchief to mop his brow. "It's going to be a hot one."

She could have told him what hot really was after being in the Outback, but she didn't want to open the conversation to an admonishment, something she found that people liked to do. Especially men who felt they must instruct the weaker sex, women who were unable to make decisions without a man. Most men weren't used to a woman being able to do what she wanted when she wanted. She knew the conversation she was about to have with Mr. Saunders was going to be a struggle.

After the cook brought a tray filled with glasses of a cool, fruity concoction, cookies, and biscuits, they settled their pleasantries and she began. "Mr. Saunders, I am concerned that Mr. Hanneman has been coming around this rental and checking on my servants."

"He has?" he asked, astonished. "Why in the world …?"

"I have no idea, but I do not wish to see the man unless it is on business. Can you make my displeasure known?"

"I most certainly will …" he blustered, angry on his client's behalf. Having a countess for a client had raised his own prestige in the Sydney community and brought him new business. Although few had met the

countess, the fact that she was in Sydney and trusted him with her affairs raised his standing.

"I would like to renew the lease for another year, but I will look elsewhere if it's necessary," she warned, both of them understanding her threat was real and the solicitor realizing that Hanneman would have to be put in his place for his presumption.

"Furthermore, I am looking to buy land," she continued, going down a mental list she had made, her plans kept in her head and not on paper. She didn't want anyone to know what she was about to do. Some would try to stop her. Some would try to beat her to it. Many would misconstrue what a woman of her stature might be doing.

"What kind of land?" he asked, wondering if Hanneman would know of some that he could acquire for this client of theirs. He would, of course, let the man know that he was not to approach the countess under any circumstances. All transactions would now go through his office; he would handle anything for her.

She told him of her needs. She wanted property near Sydney but not in the city limits, but she didn't tell him why, much to his silent exasperation. "Then, I would be interested in land further out, beyond Parramatta." She recalled the rolling hills out beyond the Nepean River and mentally smiled at how beautiful it had all been. "Something nearer to the Blue Mountains."

"Are you looking to buy a home there?" he inquired considerately, wondering at the investment in land here in Australia when she had vast estates in England. He had, of course, inquired with contacts in England about his client's holdings. She'd also sent him letters from the Outback to handle a few minor things for her while she was away visiting her friend. He found it odd that a lady of her stature had

traveled so far into the Outback for a visit. She'd been gone quite a while, and he had speculated that she might stay there.

She shook her head. "No, I was thinking something bigger. Perhaps a station?" she told him for size, hoping he wouldn't ask too many questions where she would have to hedge. She didn't like to lie, but she would to protect her plans, her children, and her intentions.

"There aren't many established stations near the Blue Mountains," he assured her, trying to remember the gossip he had heard. "Although, they would be primitive."

Remembering the rich lands she'd traveled through, her eyes gleamed at the idea of owning that raw land. "Then the land should be cheap since it hasn't been developed. I'll be looking for available land," she reiterated.

"Perhaps if you told me what these endeavors were for? I'd be able to find you more suitable …" he began, trying to rephase things so she would tell him what she was doing. He hadn't missed the vagueness of her inquiries.

"These are different uses, different transactions," she told him but would elaborate no further. She could see the solicitor's frustration building, but she would be telling him nothing more. She needed neither his opinion nor his censure to spend the vast funds available to her as the Countess of Worthington.

She was merely a caregiver of most of the funds on behalf of her eldest son, so she felt it prudent to invest judiciously. She had given suggestions and orders on the estates back in England to Sir Boardman. While she was in charge of her son's inheritance, she had her daughter and other son to provide for. The funds she used down here in Australia would be her own and to the benefit of them all. Her

daughter Agatha would have a decent dowry so she would be able to attract some of the finest men of the realm. That meant she would most likely go back to England, and Abigail wasn't certain how she felt about that. She had only begun to really know her daughter this past year and was beginning to find her quite fascinating.

Her youngest son, the Earl of Brentford, would certainly not be going back to England since there was no estate there for him. She would not have him living on the whims of her eldest son, the heir to the Worthington estates. Instead, she would plan to leave him whatever holdings she managed to build and acquire here in Australia. His earldom was in name only; no estates had come with the title she had purchased for the babe. Both her sons were earls, and while one was certain to be quite wealthy, the other would be what they made of his fortune. Regardless, she intended them both to have fine names, be well-regarded from their own endeavors and not merely from what they inherited.

"I will see what men I can find to show you lands that may suit, but I warn you how primitive it may be, going out to the Outback and seeing …" he began going on about the lands she so carelessly spoke of nearer to the Blue Mountains.

"Mr. Saunders, I don't think you realize how primitive it was on my journey into the Outback. I know what I am doing, I assure you," she told him tactfully. She knew he would worry about losing her patronage, but that he also felt it was his duty, as a man and as her solicitor, to protect her and her monies from acting foolishly. Unknowing of what exactly she wanted these lands for, he would put obstacles in her way.

As they concluded their business, he tendered her a dinner invitation, trying to draw her into society in Sydney. He and his wife would be the envy of everyone they knew if they managed to get the countess into their home. While it was known he had handled business dealings for her, the reality of actually meeting a genuine lady of the realm would go much further to garner prestige in their small social circle.

"I have just returned," she told him graciously as she rose and offered her hand. "I thank you for the invitation and look forward to a future dinner with you both." While she hadn't accepted the invitation, the offer of a future acceptance thrilled him. He kissed the back of her hand, bowing over it to do so, before taking his leave.

Abigail watched him leave, unsatisfied with the meeting. He wasn't enthusiastic about acquiring the lands for her, but only because she hadn't told him her plans. It was none of his business! While she would use his services if she could, she might have to find another solicitor if he didn't cooperate. She knew she would create a scandal if she wasn't careful since women didn't conduct business. However, she had ideas she wanted to execute and needed men to handle things for her. If her solicitor wasn't willing to cooperate, she'd find someone who was. Unable to move forward on her plans for land, she went inside to get her household in order.

Going upstairs to her room, Brodie, her personal maid, came forward and helped her out of her riding habit. Abigail knew it was quite scandalous of her not only to eat in the outfit but to have received her solicitor in it. She should have changed as soon as she arrived back at the house, but she and Agatha had both been hungry. She hadn't been willing to delay their meal for a change of clothing. She thought

about the customs and mores of England and how scandalous she was behaving. This was a new land; perhaps it was time for new rules.

Wearing a day dress, she looked critically at the outfits in her walk-in closet, knowing her clothes were already out of date. One of her many letters had been to Mrs. Waters, Mel's unlikely business partner. Mel had purchased a share of the business by buying a building and providing the ability for the seamstress to expand, and Abigail hoped to find such businesses herself to invest in. Abigail saw no reason not to use Mrs. Waters services as they both knew Mel had originally been Melissa. She had no intention of discussing *that* with the woman as she would never know if or when her servants were listening. She was still amazed that Brodie hadn't figured out what Mel meant to her or that the rugged man was actually a woman. None of the servants had questioned that she visited with her friend Mel, instead of Melissa who she had originally traveled to see.

Over the next few days, she met with Mrs. Waters. She didn't have to go to the woman's Sydney location; because of Abigail's status, the woman came to her. Mrs. Waters took her measurements and looked through Abigail's outfits—some of them were years old and still looked brand-new—and discussed the fashions she would need here in Sydney. Mrs. Waters left with a rather large order from her ladyship, pleased with her association and the recommendation from Mel Lawrence, her silent and absent business partner. That relationship had been most profitable as she expanded her business. She now had a dozen seamstresses working full time in her shop and more on consignment, and her creations were in demand by the wealthy and up-and-coming of Sydney.

Of all of the many letters she had written, the arrival of her banker, Mr. Duncan, was most welcome. They went over her finances, the letters she had written from the Outback, and his and her communications with Sir Boardman, who handled her affairs in England. She explained she would be making some rather substantial purchases in Sydney, told him some of the lands she would be looking for, and asked him to keep an eye out for such investments, but she didn't tell him the reasons for her interest nor her plans. She did mention she wasn't happy with how Mr. Saunders' attitude had chafed over her acquisition of land here in Australia. She knew she was shocking Mr. Duncan by taking an active role in her business affairs. Women simply didn't do that. Most had husbands, brothers, or fathers to handle their money for them.

"I do know of some lands that may come available from time to time," he told her, heeding her implied warning. He knew, with the funds available to the lady, she could well afford any mistakes the solicitor might think she was making. "I'll be happy to help you acquire more lands," he said happily as he accommodated one of his largest depositors. Her friendship with the owners of both Lawrence Station and Twin Station made her continued patronage with the bank of paramount importance. Their deposits in his bank were quite substantial and none of them spent very much of them beyond operating expenses. Her purchases and his help in acquiring could only endear him, his bank, and his services to her ladyship.

"I would also appreciate a recommendation for an architect as I would like to have some buildings—a home—built, eventually," she added.

Mr. Duncan smiled. It would be easy to introduce her to some of the fine men who had not only worked out their servitude to the Crown but the few who had relocated from England to establish their firms here in Australia.

CHAPTER TWO

One of her letters, one to John MacArthur, the owner of an estate called Camden Park, netted her an invitation to a garden party on his estate, and she gladly accepted. She met his daughter Elizabeth, a few years younger than herself, and well sought after. This opened a can of worms. With both Elizabeth and John introducing her into Sydney society, she was soon inundated with invitations. She accepted as many as she could, especially once Mrs. Waters began supplying her with new wardrobe items. Even her older dresses, freshly made in London but hardly worn, were out of date by British fashions, still they were a delightful surprise in Sydney.

It was Elizabeth MacArthur who introduced her to Elliott Evergreen at one of the dinner parties they went to. An odd sounding name, but a most valuable resource once she got to know him.

"I 'eard of ya of course, m'lady," he said, doffing his hat to her as he bowed. "I is friends with Dougal Frazier."

Dougal Frazier had been the man who took them out to Lawrence Station. He had kept them alive during the long trip, despite their complete ignorance of the Outback and its ways. While he had been uncouth, rude, and a bit of a savage, he had done the job—and been paid well for it. After he got them to their destination alive and unharmed, he immediately turned around and headed back to civilization.

"Mr. Frazier is an amazing man," Abigail understated. Even if he had been a taskmaster, she couldn't fault him for the job he had done. "I understand you've done a bit of exploring yourself," she said, her eyes sparkling at Elizabeth, who shared her enthusiasm about the land here in Australia. "I am hoping you might help me locate some land I'm looking for."

He perked up at the compliment and then listened intently as she told him what kind of lands she was looking for.

"Aye, thems Blue Mountains are a draw," he agreed. "You'll find some right fine land up close to them. Not many have realized how valuable it will be someday."

"Would you consent to take me out there so I could see for myself? We only traveled on current roads with Mr. Frazier, and we were in a bit of a hurry." She remembered the trip well, something she would never forget. It was also something she would never care to repeat. The trip to Mel's station, was something that would provide her stories and memories for a lifetime. Some of the places she had seen on the way, however, remained with her, some of the land something she would like to obtain for herself and her children.

"Just you, m'lady?" he asked, alarmed. He had never met a real-life lady of the realm and was quite intimidated. Her outfit was of fine linen and totally unsuitable for the more rigorous lands near the Blue Mountains.

"Well, me and my retinue," she corrected with a smile and laugh, totally charming and disarming him at the same time.

"Of course," he acceded, feeling stupid for his assumption but confused by her smile. Was she perhaps signaling an attraction to his fine self? After all, even a lady of her stature might need servicing now and again.

Before Elizabeth could whisk her away to meet other people of note, Abigail made arrangements with Mr. Evergreen to go the following week, with a plan to stay out several days and travel beyond the village of Parramatta.

With her father looking on proudly, Elizabeth played hostess to replace her mother, who wasn't feeling well. She'd stepped up admirably and was now introducing Lady Abigail to the governor.

"I missed the opportunity the last time you were in town, m'lady," he said apologetically, bowing over her hand as he kissed it.

"It's an honor to meet you, Governor," she told him politely. "I did so look forward to making your acquaintance." She took his proffered arm and led him away from the others.

He looked at her in surprise as she boldly left their hosts to speak to him alone, but he was in for more of a surprise as she told him her concern regarding Lawrence and Twin stations. "Both stations provide tons of wool for the colony," she explained as they walked amongst the MacArthur's well cultivated gardens. "I myself have decided to settle nearer to Sydney." She gestured out beyond the MacArthur Estate.

"People like those who cultivate the vast stations, and then those like the MacArthur's who own these fine lands, have inspired me." She didn't tell more than that. People didn't need to know she had escaped England to avoid her father and brother's attempts to steal her inheritance from not only her, but her children.

"You're settling here?" he asked, thrilled. His wife would appreciate that little tidbit of information, and would spread the gossip to her friends, earning prestige for knowing something about the mysterious countess. "And you're friends with the owners on Lawrence and Twin Stations? Why, that's good news. Stations like theirs and others," he too gestured to their hosts' fine grounds and out beyond, "are a credit to Australia and its colony."

"It would be a shame to lose them," she said pointedly.

"Lose them?" he asked, confused.

"Governor Darling, isn't it a fact that all lands beyond the Blue Mountains, are designated crown lands? If that is true, then the stations are merely leasing the lands, not really owning them. If that's the case, they do not pay taxes on the ownership and can pick up and leave." She didn't mention how impractical that would be, with their thousands of sheep, much less their fine homes, barns, corrals, and fencing of the vast lands.

"Leave?" he asked, aghast. His mind whirled at the idea that these stations that provided so much for the economy of their colony could suddenly be gone.

"Well, if they had ownership ..." she left off vaguely, gesturing with her hand, and then let it drop. "I do believe they wrote you," she added and then quickly changed the subject. "I myself am looking to purchase lands that I could improve. I'd like to raise some sheep and

perhaps my horses," she explained, making herself sound like a ninny, but manipulating the man on several fronts as she imparted the information.

The governor had received letters from both stations and from other grazers who worried about the crown lands designation and, as such, being open to confiscation or resettlement at any time. He knew of the large amount of money that both contributed in the form of work for many people and what was shipped to England. Besides that, numerous other operations had sprung up over the years because of stations like these. He couldn't afford to offend large land owners, and, while they didn't outright own the land, he could correct that. It would be of benefit to the crown to have these massive stations and their lease-holders and all they contributed, happy and productive.

"I believe, Lady Worthington, that wherever you may find land to build your home, we will be the better for it, having you live in our colony," he said to her charmingly as they parted. He hadn't been oblivious of her tactics or charm, and he appreciated her subtlety over the bold request to grant her friends their land. He could do it diplomatically and in a manner in which they would all benefit. If anyone ever questioned his authority to grant these requests, he could point out the amount of money that the crown would receive the benefits of taxation on the ownership that would ensure continued income from these stations.

The result was that both Twin Station and Lawrence Station and many others would receive patents on their properties, and the land was assigned to their heirs or assignees in perpetuity. This, however, would take months, and with the distance between Sydney and the stations,

they wouldn't know until the following shipment of supplies and mail from the larger city.

CHAPTER THREE

Abigail found land through the bank. It was in Parramatta, and it suited one of her ideas well. Negotiations between her, her solicitor, and the landowners, though, took a while. The property adjoined unsettled areas, and for this she could appeal to the governor directly, discretely getting a discount on the purchased crown land that would adjoin the other plots that she was negotiating on. When all was said and done, she owned quite a parcel. She immediately hired men to fence the land, many thinking that the owner, which wasn't known to them, was doing so with the intent of settling there and raising sheep or cattle. She intended to do neither.

A letter from Mr. Cherwin, the manager of her mills in England, pleased her as it answered many of her questions. He informed her that the manager he had been training, Mr. Evans, would be arriving within

two months, along with his wife and six children. He would be sending trained men when certain projects were completed, but in the meantime, Evans was a good man to start the operation she had in mind for the land in Parramatta. She looked forward to Mr. Evans' arrival. In the meantime, she had plenty to occupy her time.

"Brodie, I know how much you don't enjoy riding, so I am leaving you here, not only with the children but to help Leesa and Bonnie," she informed her maid.

"But, my lady," she went to argue, "how long will you be gone?"

"I'm not certain. We are going to look at some land that I may purchase. I don't know how long that will take."

"I thought you purchased that land out in Parramatta …" she began and then quickly clapped her hand to her mouth.

"Eavesdropping is a terrible habit," she admonished the young woman, her voice tight, controlled, and chilly.

"Yes, ma'am." Brodie curtsied and looked down at the ground.

"You're dismissed," Abigail said, turning away, not willing to discuss it further. "Make certain my bag has the same types of garments I used on the trip out to Lawrence Station. I don't want any fripperies."

"Yes, ma'am." Brodie agreed, hurrying off before she could get into any more trouble for having overheard her ladyship's private business. She'd been a fool to mention it.

Abigail set off with four of her guards, leaving six at the house to protect the children and their household. She was pleased that her captain and she had managed to hire a couple of retired soldiers to fill empty positions. Her captain of the guard had trained them, specifically for her ladyship's household and needs, knowing that they

didn't need to know the particulars of what their jobs as guards for her would entail but that they should, or would, have need of them. The four she took with her had been to Lawrence Station before, and they dressed as though they were grazers so no one would know they were guards for the Countess of Worthington. She also dressed simply, as a woman of the Outback would, with no gowns or anything to indicate she was a lady of the realm.

Elliott Evergreen was surprised at the four guards accompanying the lady. They weren't London fops as he had expected, but hardened English guards who had sharpened their skills on their first trip in the Outback. They were no-nonsense about their jobs and committed to keeping her ladyship safe. He was further surprised that Abigail was willing and able to cook over the fire.

"Mr. Frazier made sure I knew how to do this, and Mrs. Lawrence further showed me," she explained, not really discussing her time in the Outback or why she had gone there. In fact, she was tight-lipped about her plans.

She smiled as they headed out from the village, the small hill a reminder of the time they'd been this way in the past. They were riding, not her spoiled and pampered Thoroughbreds, but some of the Brumbies she'd had Clarence acquire for everyday riding. Brumbies were a mix of breeds. They were hearty, and their stamina was much more suitable for trips such as these. She loved the views as they rode down through the woodlands and outlying farms towards Prospect Hill. The panoramic sweep of the distant lands out beyond it were a reminder that she was not in England anymore. The rolling hills that led to the Nepean River and its wide valley before the Blue Mountains

was like nowhere she could imagine, not even in books, and she loved getting lost in the haze as they headed west.

She saw nothing had changed from her previous visit to the area. There were still isolated flocks of sheep and farms. The area was still huge, uncrowded, and fertile. The unique wildlife she had experienced on her trip into the Outback was here. The kangaroos, the wallabies, and even wombats that they occasionally saw. She loved the pug-like noses of the drop-bears—also known as koalas—that looked so warm and fuzzy, cuddly even, despite their long claws and sharp teeth. They ate the leaves of the eucalyptus trees as they climbed, ate, and slept. Spotting them in the trees they loved, she couldn't help but stare.

Elliot showed her a turnoff from Penrith that would take them north along some lakes at the foot of the Blue Mountains. She'd been staring at the mountains—clear today—as they rode the thirty miles or so from Parramatta. That reminded her to look into purchasing a house or two for her men coming to Australia from England, perhaps another one for herself. Although, from what she had seen, the village didn't have a lot of proper homes for someone of her stature, much less the manager she was hiring. She would look into building them instead. She would need a temporary house to stay in when she was in the area and her manager would need one for his family unless he decided to live on the grounds of the mills she was planning to build.

They traveled for a week along the edge of the Blue Mountains, experiencing some of the wildest lands she had ever seen, uninhabited except for the occasional Aborigine who stared at them in passing. White men and, especially, White women were a rarity.

"There's no getting across them mountains," Elliott assured her, nodding towards the Blue Mountains they had been skirting. "Only found the one way so far."

"You said it right there, Mr. Evergreen," she agreed pleasantly. At his odd, little look she added, "So far."

He smiled. She was quick, this one, and he wondered why they were on this sightseeing trip. She claimed she wanted to see more of Australia, but even he was feeling a little lost. He could see she liked seeing the land, the odd animals and birds on it, but wondered exactly why they were out here. On their fourth day out, she asked to return to Penrith.

"What river is that over there?" she asked, having seen the lakes and ponds and streams pouring into it from her vantage point on a large hill. Her Outback hat flapped as she nodded towards where she was indicating.

"The Nepean?" he asked, hoping she didn't want to cross it. "There is a safe crossing back in Penrith."

Ignoring his comment she asked, "And would you be able to find this area again, say on a map if you were asked?"

"Aye, I could do that," he stated, puzzled, wishing she would explain what she was after.

"This sure is beautiful country, isn't it, Mr. Evergreen?"

"Yes, ma'am, it is," he agreed.

As they seemingly meandered, he attempted to be charming. His initial thought that she might be looking for male companionship was quickly dispelled. Not by the lady herself but by her guards, who brooked no interference with the countess. He had been surprised that she genuinely wanted his expertise and knowledge about the lands they

explored. It was almost like talking to a man, the questions she asked. But looking at her, no one could confuse her for a man. He was diplomatic in his replies to her many questions, as befitted a lady.

"Damn birds ain't good for nothin'," he complained one morning as they prepared to leave camp. They watched a couple of cockatoos fighting for space amongst the trees. "Can't even eat them, not enough meat there."

"Oh, I find them lovely!" Abigail exclaimed, stopping to admire their squawks and fluttering wings. "There are so many different kinds."

He found her an odd woman, but perhaps ladies were all that way, with no knowledge about anything other than their teas and parties. He was still puzzled as to why they were out here.

"So, from Penrith, north along the Nepean, do those lakes and creeks we saw have names?"

He shrugged. "I supposed the Aborigine's have names for some of 'em," he griped, wondering at the waste of their time.

As he left her back in Sydney, he was still unenlightened as to why they had gone all that way for a seemingly useless purpose. A camping trip? She'd mentioned that once, but he had no idea. Still, she'd paid him for his time. He was, however, alarmed to be summoned by a solicitor to the magistrate's office.

"You Evergreen?" the clerk grunted, annoyed at having him before him.

"I am. I got a summons to appear—"

The clerk waved off whatever he had been about to say. "Come this way," he said instead and led him to an inner sanctum, leaving him to the men who were inside

Elliott looked around at the rich woods that lined the walls, wondering what this was about. He wasn't aware of doing anything wrong, but some officials were peculiar and he might have offended someone without even knowing it.

"You Evergreen?" a man with a poorly adjusted wig asked. Using his finger to lift some snuff from a gold container, he snorted the white powder and then brushed his cravat of the substance that fell.

"I am. What's this about?" he demanded belligerently, certain he was in trouble and not willing to go peacefully.

"You took Lady Worthington out to Penrith and beyond last week?"

"Aye, I did. Her and her guards," he clarified, starting to sweat. What if he had offended her ladyship somehow? He wracked his brain for anything he could have said or done to insult her.

"Could you show us where?" the man asked, indicating a large table where several maps were unrolled and held down with various paperweights.

He approached the table with some trepidation, worrying that somehow, he had overstepped. And with a lady, who knew what the punishment would be? He was only glad he hadn't touched her, despite his initial suspicions. He showed where they had gone on the rather primitive map, surprised there weren't more details. "We went up here and rounded here," he indicated with his finger.

"Near Koolyangarra?" another voice asked. He looked up to see another man in the room and nodded.

"Well, that's too much for anyone," yet another man murmured softly.

"But the governor …"

"Will have to trust our judgement," one of the others finished for him.

They continued their discussion for a while, forgetting about Evergreen. He didn't understand at all why he was there. They consulted him once or twice more about the lands the party had traveled through, having him show them locations on the map as they filled in details. They dismissed him after two hours, and he left, shaking his head, more confused than when he'd been called in. Had they really wanted to fill in the details on the maps? He knew there were skilled map-makers going all over Australia already. He wasn't one of them, so why had he been summoned?

CHAPTER FOUR

"**S**o, you can see, Lady Worthington, that land there is totally unsuitable as it hasn't been cleared, and the …"

Abigail waited patiently to let the man finish. She had heard from several of these *experts,* men who thought they knew better than she, a mere woman, and an aristocrat to boot, but her mind was made up. She wanted land, wide, open land that would abut the Blue Mountains, where she also wanted land. She had used Koolyangarra as a landmark because it was such a unique name, but she knew the men attempting to advise her would grasp at this Aboriginal name and be prejudiced about it. Anything Aboriginal was scoffed at, thought inferior, and not worthy of their time. None of them had ventured that far into the interior of Australia. They preferred the burgeoning city of Sydney and couldn't understand her desire to buy more land, especially land far off

into Australia. It was quite frustrating, especially when Mr. Duncan, her bank director, or Mr. Saunders, her solicitor, mentioned the Parramatta properties and suggested she build a home there. That, to them, was reasonable and an acceptable distance from Sydney.

"Thank you for your well-meaning advice," she answered back politely. "You stated there is a station here that you own?" she asked Mr. Duncan, pointing to the map. This particular station was at the base of the mountains but on the far side of the Nepean River from where she had explored with Mr. Evergreen.

"Yes, but it was so far from town that I'm certain that is why it failed," he responded pompously.

Abigail didn't remind him that Lawrence and Twin Stations and many others were much further into the interior but had succeeded. There could be a million reasons why this other station failed. "I would like to see this station and …"

"Lady Worthington … Countess," he protested, unsure of how to address her properly. She was the most exasperating woman. "I don't think …"

"Mr. Duncan, I have expressed an interest in a station that is owned by this bank, and I believe those owning shares in this bank would like to sell it." She didn't mention she had quietly purchased shares in this very bank, preferring to keep that information to herself for the time being. She knew that if anyone knew that she, a woman, had been buying up shares in businesses in Sydney, there would be a scandal. "Are you saying I cannot look at this station and perhaps purchase it if I so desire?"

"Why I, well …" he stuttered, absolutely astounded at her arguments, which were entirely correct.

"Then good, if you would be so kind as to provide me with the particulars, I think another trip is in order, and I do have to see about engaging Mr. Evergreen to escort me and my guard." She knew that going herself was quite the scandal. She should be sending her men, but she wanted to see the land for herself to make the best decision for what she was planning. Most thought she should be attending garden parties or other formal events here in Sydney. Her avoidance of several of those in the past was thought peculiar. She knew most just wanted a feather in their cap and to be able to say that the Countess of Worthington had attended their event. She was busy, something they did not understand. After attending several, she decided she didn't want her days and evenings taken up by gossiping people, who merely wanted to climb in their social status. She used the parties to obtain information, preferring to learn from the men who attempted to engage her with dancing and flirting with the pretty countess, some even attempted to court her. She attempted to glean information from the various gentlemen without them being aware of it. She couldn't do that with pointed questions as they would clam up, the conversations not being suitable for ladies. Business was not something a lady engaged in.

"You realize that the more you resist their attempts, the more gossip that will ensue?" Elizabeth MacArthur informed her with a smile. She had dropped by the house that Abigail rented to confirm that Mr. Evergreen would be available to take Abigail out again. He had been reluctant, now concerned that his association with her ladyship was being judged by those in power. He hadn't liked being summoned. Elizabeth had explained that Abigail was merely looking at the land, that those men who had questioned him were asking about things they

didn't know about. He was in no danger of being incarcerated. Besides, he could use the money that the countess was paying him.

"It won't be the first—or the last time—that I create gossip," Abigail lamented, her own smile hovering. She was grateful for this friendship with Elizabeth, one of the few who would actually understand her desire to have an estate of her own. The MacArthur estates built by Elizabeth's father were quite something. Abigail could only hope to find gardeners and other men who wanted to help her build her own.

Elliott Evergreen was not as pleased to be escorting the countess once again to the area beyond the Nepean River and up beyond the Emu Plains towards the Blue Mountains. He saw a change in his employer, however, as they approached the area of the failed station. While the station itself was nothing more than a hovel with a few outbuildings, the land was beautiful and flat for a distance, but then it gave over to rolling hills leading up to the mountains, which were full of trees with rocky embattlements sticking out prominently.

She was delighted to see the many kangaroos and various birds, still reveling in the antics of the cockatoos, and Mr. Evergreen identified another bird called a lorikeet that enchanted her.

"Mr. Evergreen, can you get the exact location of this for me?"

"Ma'am?" he asked, to be certain they were understanding each other. He had a feeling the men who had summoned him before were not going to be happy about this trip either. This time, she was

determined and he could see it. He hoped being her guide wouldn't affect his future employment; those men were very powerful and despite what Miss MacArthur had said, he wasn't certain the money would be worth it.

"I wish to purchase this station, such as it is." The property had not been cleared properly or kept up in any way, probably even when they were trying to establish it as a station. "That land," she indicated the flats up to the rolling hills, "I want to know exactly where we are so that, if it is available, I may purchase it." They looked at the run-down hovel and the buildings that were falling down about it.

"But, ma'am, this is so remote and far from …" he began, but at her look, he resigned himself. She had paid him well for his last attempt to show her available land. It hadn't suited her, but this even more remote property on the far side of the Nepean, far from recognized civilization, was going to cause an uproar. If her advisors had felt the other land was undeveloped and unsuitable, this was going to cost him any job he might have hoped to obtain. Still, he had a job to do, he had agreed to guide her, and it wasn't looking out for what this eccentric woman with too much money and no man to advise her would do. He noted down the coordinates for her, and they headed a different direction so Abigail could view more of the countryside. As they left the station, Elliot concluded he would never get another job in Sydney because of this woman and her determination. He wondered if he should travel down to Melbourne and begin casting about there, get familiar with the area.

But it was worse than Elliott thought. He was once again summoned before the banker, the solicitor, and various other men to be interrogated on where they had gone and why he had taken the countess to that area.

"You have met her ladyship. She is rather a … determined woman," he told them diplomatically. Several of them nodded, one even voicing his opinion, "she is being irresponsible." but the governor's man was there to counter all their arguments.

"It's her ladyship's money. And while she is negotiating for this … this hovel—did you call it?" he asked Elliott, who nodded. "It is ultimately her decision."

Abigail had asked the governor to look into the matter because her banker and solicitor were dragging their feet on her request to obtain the station and land that it encompassed and the additional lands around it. She'd told the governor that she wished to improve the land, providing jobs for settlers coming into the area. And while he heard and acknowledged the banker and solicitor's concerns, the governor needed this woman to be happy, or his wife, determined to be associated with a lady of the realm, would make his life miserable. He wanted to grant Abigail another favor if he could. He had already sent surveyors to Twin and Lawrence stations to establish the boundaries of both stations for land grants so that they and their heirs would own the land in perpetuity. The surveyors would go on to other stations to do the same eventually. Now, he would have to send other surveyors out to the land that Lady Worthington wished to acquire, to the station and the lands surrounding it. It would be up to her to develop it.

It all took weeks, months really, as the surveys were done, the station was determined to be abandoned, and the land around it was

verified as crown lands and available for settlement. The station, already in the hands of the bank, was ready to be offloaded to the *unsuspecting* countess, who couldn't be more thrilled to acquire it and the additional crown land.

"I do hope, Lady Worthington, that you know what you are doing?" Mr. Saunders warned her for the umpteenth time. He had advised against the purchase time and time again. It was too far from Sydney for him to observe the property, much less help her if she got into some sort of difficulty.

"I do thank you for your *help*," she said, tongue in cheek, still angry that he'd put up roadblocks in what should have been a simple land purchase. Mr. Duncan too had attempted to dissuade her repeatedly, and she wouldn't forget that. But Mr. Evergreen had been immensely helpful. She'd paid him well for his work and recommended him as one of the surveyors so that she would know the full extent of her holdings.

Evergreen was surprised to be offered this chance. Lady Abigail had provided him with even more employment. Melbourne would have to wait.

"Ma'am?"

Clarence approached her one day as she went over the architect's drawings, annoyed that she couldn't describe precisely what she wanted to the architect or draw it accurately herself. Their assumptions over what an aristocrat should have versus what she wanted were quite different, and she'd had numerous meetings with corrections she wanted made to her home. She'd seen many of these types of boring buildings back in England and in her younger days had attended parties of her friends at some of them. She wanted something different, something more … Australian if that were possible.

"My lady?"

"Yes, Clarence, what can I do for you?" she asked, looking up from the table where she was still breaking her fast. She wondered what her coachman needed.

"I have found him!" he said triumphantly.

"Him?" she asked, frowning and wondering what this was about. She'd put him in charge of the horses they had here in Australia, having brought so few from England. The couple of grooms he had trained and the few boys they'd employed were too many for the scant number of animals they had in their stables.

"Mr. O'Grady, ma'am?" he asked, worrying his cap in his hands and wondering if she were angry with him. It had taken months to locate the man. "Shamus O'Grady, ma'am?"

At the name, she recalled the conversation she'd had with her coachman a while ago to find this elusive builder who had worked for her friends. She was thrilled that he had found him. "And where is he?" she asked, delighted at this piece of good news.

"He's outside, ma'am, but um, er …" he hesitated, worrying his hat some more.

"Yes, what is it? Speak up, man!" she demanded, getting annoyed at his mumbling.

"He's um … he's …" he began again and at her angry look, quickly finished, "drunk."

"He's what?" she asked, looking at him in astonishment. She was eating her breakfast, and the man she had him seeking was inebriated?

"Apparently, he has been drinking a while, ma'am," he said apologetically, feeling really uncomfortable for having to bring this to her ladyship's attention.

"Well then, wait until he is presentable and bring him to me then," she answered, dismissing the problem as though it weren't important.

"Ma'am?" he pleaded.

"What is it now, Clarence?" she asked, looking up from her papers, excited to share them with the Irishman that both Mel and Carmen had used. She'd seen the results of his work and was hoping to get started on the buildings she wanted him to oversee for her. The months of delays due to men putting up roadblocks in her way had been aggravating.

"I don't know how to get him to stop drinking. Apparently, he's been at this for quite a while," he repeated meaningfully. "He's lost everything, ma'am." The rumors about the Irishmen were quite horrible, which was why Clarence had trouble finding the poor man. He wasn't about to repeat them to his employer. Mr. O'Grady was one step away from run-ins with the law.

"Clarence, this is the man whose brilliance built two homes that I admire. I would like to hire him for his expertise. Please see to it, whatever it takes, that he is dried out and not allowed another drop of drink so that we can proceed with the plans." She stopped to gesture to her papers. Because the plans weren't correct, she would have to rely on men such as Mr. O'Grady to ensure things were done as she wished. Plus, she was angry with her solicitor and didn't want to ask him for a recommendation for a different builder because she was certain he would send her someone, such as himself, who would not do as she wanted. The land was nearly hers, and she wanted to get started on it!

"Yes, ma'am. It will be as you wish," he said, quickly bowing his way out to rush back to the man. He found O'Grady leaning over the balustrade of the porch, retching into the bushes. "Come on you,"

Clarence said, pulling the man towards the stables. The man stumbled and staggered, barely standing on his own two feet. The coachman locked him in a stall, giving him a bucket for his bodily functions. He returned to give him bread and water, a blanket, and some hay, nothing more.

"You can't do this to me!" the Irishman ranted when he was sober enough to be coherent. Clarence ignored him and instructed the grooms and stableboys to disregard the man. On her ladyship's orders, the man was not to be released, no matter what he said.

CHAPTER FIVE

Abigail was so thrilled that Clarence had found the builder, she completely forgot the state the man was in and the order she had given her coachman. And she was so filled with the idea of building on the land she was purchasing that she repeatedly went over her notes, sub-par drawings, and ideas.

When a Mr. Evans presented himself to her a few days later, she was confused because the name sounded familiar, but she couldn't place him. Caught up with the plans on her future home, she looked at Mr. Jefferies in consternation when he announced the man as though he had an appointment.

"Who is this?"

"A Mr. Evans. He stated you were expecting him?" he asked with a note of doubt in his voice, as she obviously didn't know the man.

People tried this sort of thing all the time with the nobility, and it was his job to keep out the riffraff. With the guards about the place and their unique orders to protect her ladyship and the children, he realized he had just made an error, what if this was someone she'd instructed them to keep away? Obviously, this Mr. Evans was *not* expected, and her ladyship shouldn't be bothered with such. "I will just turn him away …" he began, starting to bow.

"Wait a moment, Jefferies," she countered, raising her hand to halt him. Something about the name Evans niggled at her consciousness as she tried to remember. "Is he from England?"

"Yes, ma'am, I believe he stated he was sent by a Mr. …" He tried to remember the name but was startled when she stood up abruptly.

"By a Mr. Cherwin?" she asked excitedly.

"Yes, ma'am. I believe that's the name he presented." Mr. Jefferies was alarmed at the young countess's excitement.

"Please, send him in immediately," she stated, seating herself once again and gathering up her papers to put aside.

"Of course, m'lady," he said, bowing himself out and going to the man who apparently *was* expected and acceptable. "Her ladyship is this way," he said loftily to the man who was waiting patiently in the atrium. Jefferies led the way back to the library and ushered the man in. "Mr. Evans, my lady," he announced, bowing himself out again and closing the door for privacy. He didn't know what this man had to do with the countess—it was none of his business—but he had left him near the guard just in case. This was the first home he had worked in that guards were a regular presence, and he knew his duty was to protect the family from unwanted visitors. He returned to his other duties, checking on the footmen and guards. He glanced

disapprovingly at Mrs. Fredericks, recently elevated to housekeeper and still learning the job. He felt he could do a better job than this former maid. He'd heard that she'd been a wet-nurse to his lordships. It simply wasn't appropriate that she rise up from that lowly position, and her son, already a pot-boy! It was presumptuous that these people didn't know their place.

"Mr. Evans, this is a pleasure," Abigail said in a delighted voice. "I trust your trip was pleasant?"

"Not really, ma'am," he said, removing his hat and bowing. "The little ones were seasick the whole way."

"Ah yes, Mr. Cherwin wrote that you have what, six children?" she asked, trying to remember what Cherwin had written about the man. "I hope the house I rented for you is adequate."

"I'm certain it will be more than adequate, ma'am," he answered immediately, leaning from foot to foot, feeling uncomfortable in his one good suit. This house was so elegant, and the hotel room he had rented for his family wasn't much more than a hovel, and they were cramped for space. "I'm hoping to get right to work for you." There had been mention of the house, a big incentive for him to take the job, and he was anxious to see it and move his family there.

"Well, I hope that you can help me there."

"Mr. Cherwin said you wanted a mill manager …" he began, a broad hint to get down to business.

"Please, Mr. Evans, have a seat," she stated, gesturing to the chair across from her. "Would you like something to drink? Lemonade? Water? Something stronger?"

"Oh no, ma'am. I never drink. It muddies the mind, and so many succumb to those spirits," he said prudishly as he took a seat. "Water

or lemonade would be fine," he stated, seeing she was waiting for his answer. He watched as she stood and pulled a long, thin tapestry. A couple of moments later a knock on the door and a head popping round showed the tapestry must be a bell pull.

"Yes, m'lady?" inquired the maid, looking at them both.

"Some refreshments? Two lemonades please."

"Yes, ma'am." The maid curtseyed in acknowledgement and hurried away, closing the door.

"Now then, are you ready to get to work?" she parroted his statement and turned to her guest, smiling at how uncomfortable the man looked in his surroundings. She had seen the mills and the conditions there in the the surrounding towns and villages, where many of the workers lived with their families. He wore an ill-fitting suit and boots that were worse for wear. He was attempting to keep his leg still, but she knew a nervous tic when she saw one.

"Mr. Cherwin trained me well to manage a mill …" he began confidently.

"I'm aware if Mr. Cherwin sent you to me, that you are more than well trained to do that work. How are you at managing other things?"

"Other things, ma'am?" he asked, sounding unsure of himself again.

"We are going to be building a mill from the ground up. Not only the mill, but the houses that our people who will work in the mill will be living in." She gestured outside the house, far off in Parramatta where she intended to build her mill, further adding to the mills she already owned in England. "It makes no sense to send the wool all the way from Australia back to England, only to send it back here once it's been made into fabrics and other things. We can do that right here. I hope you're the man for the job to help me achieve this."

His eyes were round at the enormity of the task he had been assigned. He was certain Mr. Cherwin had no idea the plans their employer had for this endeavor. "I will certainly try, m'lady," he answered, not certain he *was* the man for the job.

"We will succeed, Mr. Evans. We will succeed together!" she assured him and looked up as the maid came in carrying a tray filled with a pitcher of lemonade, two glasses, and variety of cookies. "Oh good, cook has been baking," she stated. "Be sure to send some up for the children when they have their midday meal," she advised the maid as she set down the tray and began to pour. "In fact, if cook has baked enough, could you have her box some up for Mr. Evans' children? I'm sure the tykes would appreciate the treat. He has six of them," she confided.

"Yes, m'lady," she answered to acknowledge the command and smiled.

"That's very kind of you, Lady Worthington," Mr. Evans stated, surprised at her generosity.

"I have three of my own, and I know how children always are craving sweets."

When they both had a small plate of cookies and a lemonade handed to them by the maid, Abigail came around the desk to sit on a settee, indicating another seat across from her for Mr. Evans. The maid left them to hurry out the door. Abigail sat up, her back ramrod straight as she maintained her ladylike persona. She held her glass in one hand and carefully balanced her small plate of cookies on her knee. After taking a sip of lemonade to clear her drying throat, she began, "Now Mr. Evans, this is what I want for our first mill …"

They talked for well over an hour, Mr. Evans becoming enthused at being in at the ground floor of this endeavor. He hadn't been certain, but the lady obviously had good ideas, but then she was the owner of the rather large complexes of mills back in England, and he had only seen a small portion of them. Mr. Cherwin had trained him to become manager of one of the mills there, but when this opportunity had arisen, had asked if he would interested? Knowing that Mr. Cherwin would always be looking over his shoulder, regardless of how high up in the management of the mills he would have achieved, he had grasped at this opportunity, never realizing there wasn't structure in place already.

"We will have to take a ride out to Parramatta and see the land. I've had it fenced since I purchased it, but we will have to clear a lot of the brush and build the buildings we need to our own specifications. I have a builder …" she left off, wondering if the Irishman was sober yet, having forgotten he was even found in her excitement over her home build. She didn't even know if the man knew how to build a mill. She reasoned, if he had built a barn—and Mel's were beautiful—he could build a mill. "… who should be able to coordinate what we need. Now, in the mills in England, were there things you thought we could improve …" She continued, having a delightful conversation with the man who wanted to prove his worth and justify her confidence in him.

Bradley Evans couldn't believe his luck. Not only had the mill owner paid for his family to travel with him, but she would provide them with a house. He hadn't seen it yet since it was out in Parramatta, but he knew staying in the run-down hotel in Sydney couldn't last. This opportunity was too good to be true. He would work, and work hard, to live up to the opportunity. He knew it was due to Mr.

Cherwin's recommendation, but he would show her that he was more than up to the task before them.

They made arrangements to ride out to the land the following day. He didn't know how to ride, but he wasn't going to tell her that. He hoped she wouldn't notice.

"These men travel with you everywhere?" he asked as they set out. He'd used a step near the stables to get up on the back of his horse. He was holding on to the edge of his saddle for dear life. There was nothing to hold onto with these English saddles. He looked nervously at the strongmen, the guards that protected her ladyship. They had guns worn proudly at their waists and tied to their saddles, knives, and—in one case— a sword.

"Of course, my guards go everywhere with me," she answered, sounding like the posh English lady he knew her to be. She didn't add that they alternated between the dozen she had on staff. Today two of the ones who went into the Outback with her and were quite familiar with her and her habits were with them, and there were two new ones who were in training. The others were scattered about the house and estate, anywhere they might be needed to protect the children. She'd soundly boxed the ears of one she had caught flirting with her governess and relieved another of his duties for ignoring the children. Working for the Countess of Worthington was not necessarily an easy position. She'd glanced at the two guards that stayed near the stables, keeping her valuable horses safe. She watched the mill manager carefully, certain he was not up to the thirty-mile ride to the mill site in Parramatta. "Mr. Evans, have you ever ridden a horse before?" she asked suddenly. They hadn't even gone a full block from her house.

"Ah, no, ma'am," he admitted ruefully. "What gave me away?"

"You're sawing at that poor horse's mouth," she stated bluntly, stopping her own mount to turn and look at him. The guards halted immediately, looking about. "Let's return to my stables," she stated.

"No, I should be fine, I can …" he began, certain she had found him lacking, but she shook her head and leaned over to lead his horse, capturing the reins easily and nearly unseating the man who clung to what little saddle he could grasp and finally grasping fists full of horse mane.

"We will be returning to the house," she told one of the guards, who nodded and exchanged looks with the other guards. They turned in unison, keeping her in a figurative box of their protection. They were all wearing grazer clothing to blend in, no need for the fancy livery that she provided them for more formal events. It did make quite an impression when the Countess of Worthington went to events with her liveried guards and servants.

As they entered the back of the house yard near the stables, they found an inordinate number of horses there, all led by unfamiliar men standing about and looking confused. They all looked up as her ladyship entered the yard on horseback, leading her manager's horse.

"Oh, my lady, I'm so glad you are back. These men have delivered your horses," Clarence called. He was himself leading a fine horse who looked ready to pull him off his feet.

"Ahoy there, my lady," a voice greeted her from where a man was dismounting from a rather sturdy looking horse, nothing like the exquisite and high-spirited creatures that were milling about the yard.

"Captain Scott!" she called excitedly.

"I brought you some of your horses," he announced unnecessarily. "I hope these will keep you busy and out of trouble for a time."

Abigail quickly dismounted, dropping the reins of her manager's horse to a groom who caught them, surprised. She had no need of help which was more than she could say for the poor manager, who inexpertly tried to dismount. He did nothing gracefully.

"Captain Scott, I'm so delighted to see you!" she said, and her voice genuinely told of her pleasure.

He smiled in reply. "I have a few things to discuss with you, m'lady," he told her, enacting a bow in her direction.

"If you don't mind waiting a moment, I wasn't expecting you at this time, but I should have known better." She turned to Clarence. "Can you make room for these?" she indicated the new Thoroughbred horses.

"It will be a tight fit, ma'am, but yes, we can make do for now," he told her. "And the new grooms?"

"New grooms?"

"The horses came with their own caretakers," Captain Scott put in helpfully, looking amused at the confusion.

"Ah yes, they will have to bed down in the hay or straw if there isn't room in the dorm above," she said to Clarence, pointing up to the rooms above the stables. "You'll arrange this?"

"Of course, m'lady," he told her, giving her a nod as he started sorting the horses and their grooms and getting them all into the stable.

"We will also need a carriage to take us out to Parramatta when we are ready." Her glance indicated Mr. Evans, who was still trying to stand up straight after the short ride. He looked awkward and embarrassed. She lowered her voice to impart, "Apparently Mr. Evans does not ride." Her tone betrayed none of the disappointment she felt in the man, but Clarence could tell that her assessment of the man had lowered. She couldn't fathom someone who could not ride a horse.

"Mr. Evans, please take a seat. I have business with Captain Scott," she said, addressing the man. He nodded and waved her off before making his way unsteadily to a seat underneath one of the trees in the yard, thankful to be off the horse. He breathed a sigh of relief to be on his own feet and another to sit down and relax under the trees.

"Captain Scott, if you would," she said, indicating the path to the door.

He gallantly allowed her to lead the way. She entered the house through a back door, startling servants who had thought she was gone for the day, while she led the way to the library. "Some refreshments, Jefferies, please," she told the butler, who immediately nodded and headed towards the kitchen. When they were seated in the library—the captain with a brandy in his hand—she smiled and said, "I thank you for the reports. Three ships now!" she stated, so very thrilled that their business had expanded since she was away in the Outback.

"Four now, ma'am," he corrected around a delicious draught of the brandy. "I can't tell you how worried I was when I didn't hear from you for so long," he said, his voice showing an admonishment but also a more personal concern. Meeting her had changed his fortunes so much for the better.

"Yes, correspondence from the interior of this land takes some time to reach its destination," she agreed. "So, you were the one that Mr. Elmswood entrusted with my babies?" her hand gestured out back of the house towards the stables, where a dozen of her Thoroughbreds were now being sorted and would soon reside.

"Aye, and a pampered lot of …" he began and thought better of the word he was going to use. After all, business partner or not, she was still a lady. "… horses I have never seen."

"Very valuable horses," she clarified with a smile. She'd written her manager about which horses she wanted transferred from England for a breeding program she wanted to start here in Australia. She'd thought he would argue, which he had by writing her, but she was pleasantly surprised that they were now here.

"I also took on passengers," he mentioned, gesturing to the back of the house where the manager had sat under the tree. "Nice family," he added.

"That's good to hear, I'm going to be building soon, and he will be managing those affairs," she declared without clarifying what she would be building. They continued on, discussing the shipping he had done, the new ships, and other business. It was so much better than writing letters. She always thought of one more thing after she had sent a letter on and had to wait—sometimes many months—to get a reply.

"Well, Captain Scott, I am very pleased that it is working out well for us. Go ahead and open that office here in Sydney if you can find the right manager," she stated, giving permission after their long talk. "If you find a dock we can purchase …"

"Wharf," he corrected with a smile. "A dock would be much too small."

She laughed. "I bow to your superior knowledge."

He smiled, stroking his full beard. He was pleased she had so much faith in him and his abilities. Finding captains that were both honest and willing to work for a woman hadn't been as difficult as he had thought, but he had wanted the *right* men. Her purchase of the ships had enabled them to expand in the years since they'd met, when he'd captained a ship she was traveling on. Their partnership had been very

profitable, sailing between England and Australia and back again, transporting both goods and people between the two land masses.

"I'll let you know the details," he told her as he arose from his comfortable chair. The brandy had been excellent, but since he knew the kind she imported, transporting much of it himself, he wasn't surprised.

She walked him out, signaling to one of the stable boys to bring the captain's mount to him.

"I'll be in touch, m'lady," he said as he effortlessly mounted up, lifting his hat respectfully.

"Arrange for my carriage to be brought around," she told another of the stable boys and headed to the tree that Mr. Evans was sitting under. "I'm so sorry to keep you waiting," she told him sincerely, having forgotten about him as she visited and concluded business with the captain. She saw that someone had provided him with water. "We should plan to stay out overnight in Parramatta if you'd care to send a message to your wife?"

Startled from his daydreaming, he stood up and bowed slightly to her. "Of course, m'lady, that would be proper to alleviate her worries." He wasn't about to tell her no, but he was disappointed that they couldn't just ride out there and back. He had had no call to ever learn to ride a horse. Living in town, he had relied on his own two feet or a hired driver on the rare occasions it was necessary. He couldn't tell if she was disappointed in him or not, but he really needed this job. With Mr. Cherwin's endorsement, he had decided to move his entire family all the way out here, and he'd be in a fine state if she found fault with him or his work and dismissed him.

Abigail quickly arranged for one of the stable boys to take Mr. Evans's wife a message, and when Clarence came up, driving the carriage himself, she allowed herself to be handed in and had Mr. Evans sit across from her.

"Ma'am, some clothing and supplies for you," Brodie said, coming up with a satchel and a basket.

"Good thinking," she complimented her maid as she placed them in the carriage for her. She nodded to her as Clarence started them out, the four guards on horseback alongside the carriage.

"Mr. Evans, have you ever been out of England before?" she asked to make conversation. She could see he was rubbernecking, looking everywhere at once and not really seeing anything. It amused her, wondering if she had been like that when they started out for Lawrence Station.

"No, ma'am, I ain't, um, haven't ever been beyond the mills and the area around them all me life," he told her, wondering if she would hold this against him.

"Then how will you know how to build the mill that I need?" she asked, concerned.

"Traveling has nothing to do with my knowledge of what should be in a mill," he told her sincerely. He then went on to tell her how he had grown up as a boy in the mill, doing errands and cleaning under the big machines, to working his way up to management. "I've run every one of them machines at one time or another," he confided, hoping he was making a better impression than he had that morning.

Having seen the children in those mills, she was horrified at the thought of a child, any child, working in them. She had told Mr. Cherwin that she didn't want children working in any of her mills.

That reminded her to write to him and ask about the new mill purchases they had discussed so long ago when she had visited the site back in England. She knew from his letters that he had proceeded with the purchases, including the dyeing plant they had discussed, but she hadn't received any status reports on them. She brought her attention back to Mr. Evans's recitation about his qualifications.

"What is that?" he asked as a bird flew low and nearly took off his hat. He put his arm up to fend it off in case it attacked.

"I believe that was a cockatoo. They are native to this land and quite profuse. You will see flocks of the various birds. Some of them are quite colorful," she enthused. "Some of them can be quite amusing."

"I'm looking forward to it, and I hope my children enjoy them as well," he told her sincerely, hoping that was the right answer. He desperately wanted to try this position and prove to her that he could do it. It sounded like it was going to be more, much more than he had been led to believe, but perhaps Mr. Cherwin hadn't realized the extend of her ladyship's plans.

They passed the hours in the carriage mostly in silence, except for when she wanted to bring something to his attention. Sometimes it was a building; other times it was a field or a tree. "I would like the mills to have a pleasant atmosphere. It was so dirty and depressing with mill upon mill in the city. We will leave some trees and not clear-cut the site, but we will also plan parks for the employees and their families to live in so they will want to work for us," she explained.

"We won't want to be too generous," he cautioned, thinking of the expense.

"Whyever not?" she asked in her pearliest of tones. "If we treat them right, they will want to stay. Their children will want to work for us when they come of age. We will want them to be happy and satisfied."

"They should be happy and satisfied with a decent wage and a good place to live. It ain't, um, isn't our job to provide them with much more. We can use that money to build more mills."

"Mr. Evans, Australia is not England, and we shall attempt to build it in the manner in which I've indicated. I want happy people, eager to earn their wages and to deserve the homes we shall build for them to live in. It isn't like England, where we will be crammed in together. There is so much more room here," she told him, her arms encompassing the vast lands around them. "We will want them to realize how privileged they are to work for us."

He nodded contemplating, surprised that she had thought of the people who would eventually work for them. He hadn't really thought of the worker. They earned their pay, and after that, it was up to them to pay their bills and make their own homes. He himself had worked and worked hard to get to this point and manage a mill. Mr. Cherwin had been reluctant to let him go, but her ladyship's letter had indicated she wanted one of his best. Mr. Evans had been proud to be considered. This obviously was a different viewpoint than what he'd been taught, but he was willing to comply. Perhaps the lady was correct.

He was surprised when she politely inquired after his wife and children, asking how they were after the long trip by sea. Thinking she was asking specifically about how old his children were, he said, "Me three oldest are almost ready to come work in the mill. By the time we

have 'em built," he indicated the lands where they would be building the first of the mills, "they should be able to work for you." He could see immediately that he'd said something wrong when her face became thunderous.

"Mr. Evans, there will be no more children working in the mills owned by the Worthington family, and that includes those here in Australia." Seeing his shocked look she added, "Am I clear on that? No children working in our mills?" At his nod, she looked away, ostensibly to look out over the lands they were passing, but inside she was writing a letter to Mr. Cherwin asking specifically if he had enacted that particular edict for their mills in England. She knew it would be a hardship for some families who put their children to work as early as they could to get their wages, but there were other positions that they could do and not in the dangerous mills where they could be maimed or killed.

It was quite late when they arrived at the land and made camp. Evans was surprised as Clarence and the countess made dinner from the supplies that had been put in the carriage. Two of the guards gathered wood for the fire they made.

"Mr. Evans, my maid has packed you a blanket to sleep with," she said, handing him the extra. She knew Brodie had packed her too much, and it was a good thing because no one had packed the poor man anything. He certainly didn't have a change of clothes with him.

"Thank you," he said gratefully, feeling a bit chilled and not just from the night air. There wasn't anything around for miles, and it surprised him that this was where she was planning on building her mill. The land felt different from anything he had seen back in

England. There was also something in the air, something he couldn't define that definitely felt different.

"How is Mr. O'Grady doing?" she asked Clarence as they got a dinner for the seven of them. The guards were sitting in a square around them, looking off into the dark rather than at the fire.

"He's right salty," he admitted with a grin. "But he hasn't had a drink in a while, and I hope he will stop his belligerence. He weren't happy with us," he further admitted.

"I can imagine." She laughed and began dishing up food for her men. Surprised that the countess would serve them, the men hastened to their feet to eat standing up.

"Oh, Lady Worthington, this isn't necessary," exclaimed Evans who got up from the log he had been sitting on, staring into the fire.

"Well, if you're going to eat, it is," she teased, handing him the plate and then scooping up one for herself. Clarence had helped himself once he saw she was fed. They talked of England—the coachman who was now stablemaster, the mill manager, and the lady—each talking from their own perspective and sharing what they missed from England. Abigail added about what she had found in comparison in Australia and how much more there was available if the right person found the right place. "I think that England was so established, so set in its ways that we can do more here. There is so much more land."

"You don't think you will ever return to England, ma'am?" Evans asked, surprised, as he finished his meal. He had never thought to speak to a lady of the realm, and yet she seemed like a well-brought up woman, and not part of the ton to him in her ways. He would not have dared speak to her unless she spoke to him first. Now, she not only spoke to him, but expected him to converse with her. She sat on a log,

eating with the rest of them, even serving them, something he never thought he'd see.

"Maybe someday," she mused. "My oldest son, the new lord, will, but I'm building for here, for now, and I've seen some things that Australia could use." She thought of Mel and how she had built from nothing, and now her station was so vast. She didn't want something like that, but then she thought of the MacArthur's and their beautiful lands and thought something more like that would be useful for her horses. Thoughts of Mel made her remember that she had diversified her holdings and even invested in that seamstress' business that she was able to finance and keep her anonymity. "My youngest son may wish to run the Australian holdings, but my daughter will probably end up back in England with her brother."

Both men nodded. It made sense. Although owning such large plots of land was beyond them. They were working men and took their orders from such as she. They could only imagine what her properties in England were like, and as Evans had seen the mills and Clarence some of the stables, they only had a small idea of how much she owned.

That night Abigail missed the extra blanket she had given the manager, but she burrowed down in her own blankets, having changed her clothes to something a little warmer and cleaner since Bonnie provided them. She changed again in the morning, wearing a new dress as they drove around the property on the road built to erect the fences and property lines.

"So, as you can see, Mr. Evans, we have plenty of land in which to grow. But I'd like to get started as soon as possible on the one mill. I am hoping Mr. O'Grady will be well enough to start this with his men

and you can direct him where you want things. We will need to order some things for the mill from England and have Captain Scott ship them in for us." She showed him her rough drawings of not only the mill but the houses for their employees.

"Aye, m'lady," he answered, finding it easier to go along with her and her many plans. He was a simple man and couldn't fathom all the ideas she had rolling around in her head. It was too much for him. However, when it came to the mill, he was certainly able to hold his own and talk intelligently about it all and what they would need.

"Some of those things will take many months to order and ship them here," she concluded, gesturing to the land they were viewing. "We don't want anyone to know what we are about until we are ready to take on some of the wool that travels through this great country." She thought of the massive piles of wool from Mel's shearing and guessed an equal amount would probably come from Twin Station.

Mr. Evans nodded, finding it easier to go along with whatever she said, knowing that if he questioned anything, he might show his ignorance. However, he could tell her about the latest machines they would need for the mill.

"We will now go to the house I rented for you and your family so you can see if there is anything you need to bring with you from Sydney when you move out here. I will provide you and your family a wagon to bring your things out so you can get started on hiring some men to clear some of the brush from this. You can probably use some of the same men who put up the fences and built the roads." She indicated the land she owned. "Just remember I want trees for shade and parks for the children living in those houses you are going to have built. We may need shade for the mill as well," she said, indicating

some of the absolutely huge eucalyptus trees that grew in such abundance. There were so many different kinds of trees, but she was fascinated by all the different kinds and proud of the ones she already knew the name of.

He nodded, already thinking ahead to that, wondering if this Mr. O'Grady would know people he could hire or if he knew someone that could assign men from the prisoners who worked out their sentences. Hiring some of the men who had already done some of the work made sense as well.

Abigail must have read his mind. As Clarence drove them to the house she said, "I'll ask the governor to send men to come out here and work with you, getting started on the site with Mr. O'Grady. I expect the two of you to get a good start on the mill and then the houses. And any of the men who show promise we can promote."

He nodded, numb from all the ideas she had bombarded him with, but he had taken notes, having learned to read and write because of Mr. Cherwin.

The house was more than adequate, the rooms large, and he knew his wife and children would be thrilled. The hovel they had been living in, the hotel, was not something he wanted to stay in long term and this house was more than double the size of the small cottage they had lived in back in England. He'd only managed the cottage because of his position thanks to Mr. Cherwin and all he had taught him over the years; otherwise he'd have been in one of those dismal houses common mill workers lived in. He wondered if it was because Australia was so big and had so much more room that they built accordingly. He adjusted his way of thinking as he understood more of what Lady Worthington wanted on the initial mill he would be building. Thinking

back to the dilapidated hovels the workers lived in, he could see why her ladyship wanted better.

The village surrounding the house was small, but he could see it growing, thriving even, and with the added influx of workers he would be hiring, it showed promise.

"Will this do?" she asked, worried and wondering if she should have just purchased the house instead of renting it for her manager.

"Oh yes, m'lady, this is wonderful!" he enthused, showing the first signs of his delight at the position he found himself in. He'd been very intense as they went over the plans for the mill, trying to concentrate on all she wanted done. There was so much to take in, and this was an unfamiliar land and the work she would have him do.

"Well, if this is adequate for you and your family's needs," she said, handing him the key that she'd obtained from the landlord when she'd rented it for a year, "then let's return to Sydney and get started. I'd like to get back before it gets dark."

He did too, having not liked his one night of camping out. He'd been cold by turns and heard odd sounds coming out of the darkness. She'd warned him that getting used to new places would take some time and not to let his imagination get away from him. He'd dismissed it as women's vapors, but he now wondered if he had imagined those noises in the dark. He much preferred having people around him, and the house in town would provide that. He wouldn't be staying out at the mill site at night. He also thought his wife would prefer having neighbors she could gossip with.

They managed to return to the countess's rented house before sunset, but Mr. Evans had to make his way to the hotel in the dark. One of the guards went with him so that he would know where to send

the wagon in the morning to collect the Evans family and their things. In a strange city and worried about being mugged,. Hal Evans was never so glad as to have the guard with him on the way back to the shabby hotel.

"See you in the morning," he assured the guard, tipping his hat. They hadn't spoken much, the guards not willing to talk much around their lady, who they were assigned to protect. She didn't invite friendly conversation as they had their duty.

"You've been gone so long," Evans wife greeted him, running into his arms.

"Shhh, don't fret," he told her, smiling over her shoulder at his wide-eyed children. "We've got a beautiful house that m'lady has provided for us, and I'll get to work immediately so she'll be happy with my work."

"A whole house?" she asked dreamily. "Oh, Hal!"

"There's a plot of land around the place too," he added, watching the delight on her face.

"They'll be happy," she said, indicating the children. The hotel had been cramped quarters, and she'd worked hard at keeping them quiet, not wanting to upset the keeper with all the many children, but it had been difficult.

"Aye, and you'll have to find out from the neighbors what kinds of plants will grow in that garden you're already planning," he teased, giving her a final hug before setting her back. He turned to the children. "Have your things ready to go first thing. Lady Worthington is providing us with a wagon to transport us to our new home."

"Really, Father? A home of our own?" one of his older daughters ventured to ask.

"Yes, it will be a little bare at first, but I'm certain we will find things to furnish it with," he said, looking at them all with a big smile. He didn't mention his fears or the noises at night or how far from everything Parramatta was, but he hoped, in time those fears would dissipate. He also didn't mention the school that her ladyship had stated she wanted to find a teacher for all the children whose parents would work in the mill. If the children were going to work in the mill, he couldn't see the point of schooling, but since her ladyship didn't want them there, he supposed they would have to go to any school that she set up for them. He realized working for her ladyship directly would be a lot different than when he had come up in the mills her husband had owned.

CHAPTER SIX

"Ye ain't got no right," O'Grady bellowed as Clarence fished him out of the stall he had been locked in.

"I need this stall for the horses; they're worth more than your hide," he grouched back at the stinking man. "You need to wash up before you present yourself to her ladyship." He helped guide him, pulling him by the arm out into the stable yard.

"I didn't ask—" he began, but he was blinded by the brilliant sunlight.

Clarence helped him along to a full water trough and dumped him in.

Shamus came up spitting mad, the water streaming off him. "What'd you have to go do that for?" he asked angrily, ready to fight the man.

"You ain't fit to lick the lady's boots, much less be presented to her. Wash up. I'll find some clothes you can wear!"

Shamus saw there was soap, even shaving soap, a razer, and a leather to strop it against, along with a mirror. He quickly began to peel off his soaked clothes, dropping them besides the trough, never more conscious that he was out in the open and anyone could come upon him at any time. When he was naked, he washed everywhere he could reach, but as he was looking in the mirror to see how long his beard was, a giggle alerted him that someone was stealing his clothes.

"Hey, bring those back!" he roared, lunging up to reach for them but he was too late. He ducked back down into the cold water of the trough to hide himself.

"She was instructed to wash them out for you so that you have a second set of clothing," Clarence informed him, setting down folded and dry clothes. "These should fit you in the meantime," he stated. "You *are* going to shave, aren't you?"

"I was just thinking about it," he admitted, his hand stroking the stubble that never seemed to get long enough to grow a fine beard. He sighed. Sober or not, he needed to clean up properly. It had been a long time since he'd bathed, and he couldn't remember the last time he had clean clothes much less extra.

Clarence had one of the stable boys throw the slop bucket that O'Grady had been using down the dunny. They'd emptied it a few times during the man's imprisonment, but it was a distasteful job and only someone low in the hierarchy of servants was assigned the job. Next, they removed the straw and blankets the man had slept on, the blankets going to be washed along with the threadbare and filthy old clothes the man had been wearing. When Clarence saw O'Grady in

clean and freshly laundered clothes and nicely shaved with his hair combed, he was surprised that the man looked almost dapper. Even the way he walked was jaunty. Clarence nodded and asked, "Would you care to sit down to a proper meal before you meet with her ladyship?"

"Aye, I would," he admitted, his hand rubbing bare chin, unused to being this clean in a long time. After a fine bit of roast beef, some vegetables, and a glass of lemonade—which he screwed up his courage to drink—he was escorted to the library where Lady Worthington worked her accounts. He was accompanied by Clarence and a guard who eyed the man distastefully. Despite O'Grady's being cleaned up, the guard had seen him at his worst, and with the prejudice against the Irish, he couldn't help his grimace at the man.

"Mr. O'Grady," the countess began pleasantly.

"What right do you have to hold me prisoner?" he demanded angrily.

"That's no way to talk to a lady of the realm!" Clarence hissed, grabbing the man's arm. The guard made a gesture as though to throw the Irishman out.

Amused, Abigail looked at the Irishman. "Well, I wasn't aware we were holding you prisoner." She glanced at Clarence, who looked surprised for a moment before nodding slightly to take the blame. "However, I thought you'd want to be sober for the work I'd like to discuss with you."

"I ain't got no work and no tools no more. Lost them all," he mumbled, still angry but cowed by the guard and the stableman who had imprisoned him because both were big men.

Abigail contemplated this for a moment. "So, you've lost everything?"

"Aye, I did," he said, his belligerent tone returning. His eyes darted around the room, anywhere other than the woman in front of him. His face flushed in shame to have such a lady talking to him and him, having nothing to show for himself.

"That's too bad because I have a house, some barns, and a mill I'd like you to build for me," she told him. "Oh, and some housing for my men too," she added almost as an afterthought.

"I ain't got no tools or men," he told her, looking around at the richly appointed fixtures in the room, from the books to the draperies, but anywhere other than the woman he was standing before.

"If you were provided the opportunity, as you were on Lawrence and Twin Stations, would you take it?"

Surprised at the mention of the two stations, he stood there dumbly for a moment as he considered. "What'd you have in mind?" he finally asked.

Abigail nodded to Clarence and the guard, and they both retreated to the hallway, carefully closing the doors behind them. She talked about the plans she had drawn up for her house and the barns she wanted built similarly to the ones he had built on Lawrence Station, only larger and more extensive. Then she spoke of the mill and the housing she would provide for the families of mill workers.

"That's an awful lot for one man to work on," he told her as he looked at her sketches. They were almost child-like because she wasn't a great artist, but he got the gist of it though and knew he could do the work. It wasn't the first time a client had given him such basic sketches.

"Well, I could ask the governor for help in the form of prisoners working off their indentured servitude, or would you prefer us to work with freemen?"

He peered at her out of the corner of his eye, surprised that she had that kind of pull, that she could *just ask* the governor for such a favor. Everyone had referred to her as Lady Worthington, so he decided she must be someone important. He rubbed his face and contemplated the massive buildings she wanted built and how he would go about building them.

"You'd have to start on the mill and the houses at the same time, and I think I'd want a combination of freemasons and then those working their time off," he began hesitantly, "but where would we get the tools and …?"

"I'm certain we could arrange that through the governor's office, and they can advise you on where to get the men and then everything we need. The land will need clearing, but I don't want it clear-cut. I want trees for shade and picnicking. My manager, Mr. Evans has gone out to Parramatta to start on that. I expect you to work with him. He will be the new manager of the mill and can tell you what he needs. Once that is far enough along that it can continue the design you and I agree on, you could start on my new home." She indicated the other sets of drawings.

"That's a big house," he began and traced some of her scratching's. Of course, if she were a lady of the realm, she would expect a grand house. "What's that in aid of?" he asked, pointing at some features she had scribbled.

"I would want a secret passage between the buildings, to the barns, etc. In times of old, it was thought that such might be necessary, and I

always found it intriguing that there were secrets within the houses. On my home, I want tunnels, and secret passages, and I don't know how you'll achieve that with the men you'll have working for you. But I would be delighted if you did so." She looked like a little girl excited at getting a treat.

He smiled slightly, imagining what she was describing, having seen such back in Ireland and again in England before he came to Australia. He had never thought to build it himself but knew, with a good think on it, he might be able to achieve the results she wanted. "I'm really not in any shape to …" he began to turn her down. He had to be honest with her.

"Mr. O'Grady, you're sober for the first time in how long?" She held up her hand so he wouldn't answer her. "You've lost everything by your own admission." She spread her hands out at the childish drawings she had shown him. "I've seen your work when you do the job properly, and if you do as good a job for me as you have for my friends at Lawrence and Twin Stations, I will set you up again. And after my jobs are done, I will recommend you to people where you can make a lot of money." She gestured again at the paperwork between them. "This job will require you to stay sober during its entirety. If you cannot do it, if you cannot remain sober to do the excellent job I require, then tell me and I will seek out other builders."

Shamus considered her offer, his hand stroking his chin where the beard had stood just an hour or so ago. He had nothing else to lose other than his life. He'd liked working at both of those stations, but they had kept him from the rum, especially on Lawrence Station. Mel Lawrence had scared the crap out of him when he attempted to sneak more than his share of rum at the end of a week, but it was the station

owner's wife and her odd looks that reminded him of the scary stories his mother had told him about the banshee's as a child. He wanted that job done so he could return to civilization. Being in the Outback for years had been quite the experience. This job—these jobs actually—would be quite demanding. He glanced at the countess, wondering how much of a taskmistress she would be. He slowly nodded. "Aye, I'll do it," he found himself agreeing.

"Good, then you can start immediately. I will require drawings. And you'll have to tell me how many men you will need so I can write the governor?"

He was startled, he had thought he would have some time before starting the job, but apparently not. She wanted him to start immediately. He recalled the days when you didn't need an architect for the drawings she would require. He knew of a man who could take what they had spoken of and draw plans up quickly for her ladyship. They would incorporate what the architect had drawn, modify them, and present them to get the permits to build. He could add in the hidden items later, when no one was looking so closely at his work. He had a few ideas already percolating in his mind, her ladyship having given him an incredible opportunity.

"Mr. O'Grady, this is my business," she gestured to the drawings for the mill, "and this will be my home." She indicated the other drawings. "I'm anxious to get started and see the results of your work."

He nodded. "I ain't got anywhere to stay …" he began musingly.

"Then, you can sleep in my stable until such time as you have the supplies and equipment and the men to take them out to Parramatta and join Mr. Evans. I expect that will be a short time?"

He nodded and then surprised them both by asking, "Could I have some paper and pencils to draw out more of what you want here? That way we both know what you might be wantin'."

Abigail, having gotten what she wanted, discussed finances with the man. He would not be paid for his work until he finished the jobs, other than living expenses, including room and board, and only when they were done. If he violated their agreement by drinking, even a drop for however long it took to finish the jobs, then he forfeit his salary. She would pay for tools him and his men, and he would own the tools after the jobs were completed. O'Grady reluctantly agreed to everything and sat down at a table with blank paper and pencils to sketch out what she had asked for. Abigail wrote out their agreement, signed it, dated it, and then had Shamus O'Grady sign it as well, stowing it away on her person.

Abigail went to play with her children and left O'Grady there with the door open so the guard could watch him and escort him back to the barn.

CHAPTER SEVEN

"Lady Worthington has asked for what?" the governor asked. One of his men had brought her proposal to have prisoners work on a large warehouse and some houses she was building in Parramatta.

The man explained, the wording seeming odd to him, but then she was a lady and perhaps that is how they spoke and wrote. He did mention that one of her men was hiring freed men to work out there too, and they wondered how large of a warehouse she was building. "She does offer to pay for the men that are prisoners as they work off their sentences."

The governor was still eager to stay in her good graces, acceded reluctantly to her demands. He restricted it to men who had worked on various buildings around Sydney and were due to be released in the next few months. Perhaps they would be eventually hired on by her

ladyship for whatever endeavor she was having the warehouse constructed. He wasn't privy to her dealings, but he was quite curious. Knowing she had powerful connections here in Sydney and back in England, he provided what help he could. He had been contacted in the many months since she had returned from the Outback by a man by the name of Sir Boardman, and upon checking on the man, had immediately complied with any and all of her ladyship's odd requests. The woman had far too many powerful acquaintances back in England that the governor couldn't afford to offend.

Abigail, realizing that she must develop friends in the rather small community that was the elite in Sydney, had accepted more invitations to parties, both tea and formal. She was keeping Mrs. Waters and her staff quite busy as she ordered more dresses so that she didn't appear in the same frock too often. She'd also referred several ladies to the establishment, giving Mrs. Waters even more clients. The seamstress was talking about opening a second establishment, having written Mel about the expansion in another part of the city and asking for her thoughts, and her financial input on the matter. Their accountant had written as well, confirming the income was more than adequate for such an endeavor.

Meanwhile, several people privy to local gossip asked her what the warehouse she was building in Parramatta was for and why her men were hiring so many builders. She just smiled and said they would all know in time. "My men need good artisans, and I'm certain they will find them from those settling in and around Sydney." She didn't mention the prisoners, who really had no choice in the matter, that were being sent to work for Mr. Evans and Mr. O'Grady.

"How goes the property out beyond Parramatta?" she asked the governor's man, wondering when her patent for the property would be final.

"I believe the bank already sold you the station?" he returned, hedging.

"Yes, they did, however I'm asking about the other property surrounding it that I wished to acquire."

He smiled, almost patting her hand. "That takes time, and I'm certain you will want—"

"It's been months my, good man," she cut in, tired of his condescending tone, "and whatever you are certain of, I would like to know that I owned the land we discussed," she said, eyeing him distastefully. The governor and his wife were making their way over, so she made certain to time her next phrasing correctly. "Do you treat all the people wishing to purchase land from the crown this way, or am I being singled out?"

"What's this?" the governor asked, coming up beside them and hearing her question.

"Oh, Lady Worthington," his wife interrupted. "Thank you for sending Mrs. Waters. The dresses she came up with are divine."

"I'm happy to hear that. A friend of mine is a silent partner with her and enabled her to move to that location. All those seamstresses, and she is so busy!" Abigail pretended to gush before fixing the governor with a look. "Governor," she said, holding her hand out for him to kiss.

He took her hand in his and bent over it, willing to oblige her ladyship.

"I was just talking with your man here." She indicated the now embarrassed man, who had been caught out, talking disrespectfully to

the lady. "The bank sold me that station that they had, but I'm wondering about the patents on the rest of the land?"

The man looked decidedly uncomfortable at this. Then, the governor's wife spoke up, "Surely the paperwork can be hurried along for her ladyship?" She looked beguilingly to her husband in her inquiry.

The governor smiled, neatly outmaneuvered by this woman and appreciating it. She hadn't begged, she hadn't demanded, she had merely asked. Granting her the land would cost him nothing other than a favor, and the monies they would receive in taxes in the future as she improved upon it were good for the colony. "I'm sure we can," he said meaningfully to his man.

"Wonderful, and you and your wife will be among the first visitors once my house is built, won't you?" she asked ingenuously.

"Oh, I would love that," his wife stated, clapping her hands. She was so in awe of Lady Worthington. "What will you be naming your estate, Countess?"

"It will be called Brentford after my second son. He is Lord Brentford even though the Brentford's back in England no longer have an estate. By establishing one here for him, he will have lands almost equal to his brother's back in England."

"So, your older son will inherit his paternal lands, and your second son his maternal lands, eh?" the governor quipped with a grin.

"Something like that," she agreed with a smile, not including the mill or the other buildings she intended to invest in for their whole family. What she did with her personal funds would in no way affect the Worthington estates in England or their many holdings.

"I saw one of the horses you had brought over here. How can you control such beasts?" Maisy the governor's wife asked, sounding fearful.

"I was raised on such Thoroughbreds. A friend of mine, Melissa Lawrence—you know Lawrence Station?" she asked the governor, who nodded. He had sent them the documents for ownership for the land they claimed out in the Outback once the surveyors had finished. "She and her father used to buy them; that's how I met her," she began and then thought to add, "and her brother." She might as well keep Mel's identity a secret. It wasn't like the *brother* and *sister* would ever be in the same room at the same time.

"So you intend to raise them here as well?" she asked, intrigued and frightened at the same time.

"Australia has such potential, and why not raise our own superior stock here?" she asked, raising her glass to salute her idea before taking a sip.

Maisy questioned her long enough to later provide others with gossip, especially at the gatherings that Lady Worthington did not attend. The governor and his man learned some information they had sought, about the horses just by letting Maisy gossip with the countess. They still didn't know why she needed so many men in Parramatta, but many of the prisoners they had mustered for her would indeed stay on to work for the Irishman and the English manager her ladyship had hired.

CHAPTER EIGHT

Abigail loved riding her horses, and she often took a second one to ride back from Parramatta so the sixty-mile round trip could be completed in one day if she wished. She spent many a night camping out, sitting around a campfire, under tents to keep out of the weather, until a house was built to accommodate her and her children as she watched the first of her mills being built at the site. Her legs hated her for it, but riding astride, with a wide skirt that hid the fact that she was doing so, allowed her to stay in the saddle all day. The building site in Parramatta was coming along. Already five houses were being put up, and the amount of work on the mill was astounding. It had taken months to get to this point, but the rainy season was coming, with O'Grady insisting he could get a roof on before the rains became too

much to work outdoors. That way they could work indoors on both the houses and the mill.

Discussing one of the reasons for their slow progress, he said, "It's this lumber though, ma'am. The saw pits are a piss-poor place to work. Pardon my language, ma'am." Sweating and wiping his dry mouth, he craved a drink. He often thought longingly of the rum his men indulged in each week after they had been paid. Even the prisoners got a ration of rum, and despite it being low-grade alcohol, it smelled heavenly to him. He knew though that Mr. Evans and others had been set to watch him, so he stayed far away from the drink. He also knew he was doing the most important work of his life, and if he didn't stay sober, he would never get another chance like this. Losing everything, his business, his tools, his jobs, and his reputation had really been a shock to him that he had nearly ended up in prisoner garb himself. Working for her ladyship was his last chance.

"What would it take to set up a lumber mill?" she asked instead, ignoring his course language and thinking only of their buildings. She could see where a second mill would go eventually.

"Someone with knowledge and then, of course, the workings."

"Well, I'd be willing to set someone up in business if they would be willing to set up two sawmills for me," she told him, looking at the men in the pits who held the poor end of the saw, the wood dust raining down on them, smothering them in it. It looked to be a miserable place to work. She couldn't imagine what it was like, but seeing it made her want to change the situation.

"Two sawmills, ma'am?" he asked, frowning and wondering at her ideas. He'd found her amazingly perceptive, as intelligent as the women he had met in the Outback who had recommended him for this

job. Meeting all of them had changed his perceptions on women forever.

"We need one here in Parramatta," she nodded at the sawpit before them, "and one nearer to where my station is going to be built," she explained, gesturing out beyond the mill he was building. "I don't want one on the place, of course, but near enough that you can utilize some of these trees," she indicated some of the mighty eucalyptus and other trees they'd to cut down to make room for the mill. All of it was virgin wood, having been growing for hundreds of years. She'd particularly asked that they leave some of it for the park-like atmosphere she wanted on the grounds. He knew better than to take down more than they needed because she'd been particularly upset by those who had tried to clear-cut. Not wanting to lose her favor, he'd been much more careful about what they cut.

"I'll listen up and ask around," he promised, and that was how Lady Worthington became the co-owner of a wood mill in Parramatta. A silent partner, she purchased the workings from a gristmill that had gone under in Sydney, the former owner promising he could reuse the workings for a sawmill and set it up in record time, with the help of those willing to work for him when their days were done at the jobsite with O'Grady. They didn't realize they were working for her ladyship again, but they appreciated the extra work and money. Many of them were former convicts, granted their freedom after working off their time and learning a trade. Some who had worked off their conviction had gone back to Sydney and worked on the governmental buildings that were going up everywhere, but those that stayed and loved the Outback, even the beginnings of the Outback, appreciated their freedom and the wages they could earn. A select few who saved up

enough had sent for their families as more housing became available in the area.

"Surely you won't use just wood to keep those people warm," she had commented about the workers' housing, and the next time she visited she saw masonry covering the wood frames of the houses and even the mill to keep them from the elements. The rains were coming, and Abigail knew that would keep her indoors. She wasn't looking forward to that season, but she did want to spend more time with her children when she was forced to stay in. She hadn't brought them out here to the mill site too often. It was just so much work, with all their attendants and guards. None of the children could ride for that length of time, so she had to use her carriage. She saved the lumbering coach for visits within the city and for when she needed to make a statement at the various parties and gatherings that she, as the Countess of Worthington, would attend.

Lady Worthington was a familiar sight riding on the road from Sydney; her fine horses being trotted along as her men struggled to keep up on their own mounts to keep her guarded. The riffraff stayed far away from her, anyone intending ill to the lady knowing that these men would shoot to kill to protect her. One such man had learned the hard way. He wasn't shot but skewered on a sword he hadn't even seen coming as he attempted to accost the young countess. Why he had done it, perhaps thinking she was alone and vulnerable and not seeing her guards, they did not know. Abigail had vomited over the incident, but she'd been assured by the governor himself when he learned of the incident that the man had gotten what he deserved. Patrols were increased, and the soldiers became a bit more belligerent towards those

old lags who were no longer prisoners but hadn't prospered upon their release.

At one of her garden tea parties, she was admiring the roses, gifts from people who raised them back in England and some native species she wasn't familiar with. She was thinking of the gardens she had seen at Elizabeth's home and those she would want to plant at her own home. She hoped her hostess would condescend to give her cuttings.

She overheard two women she didn't know talking about *iron horses* being built. Anything with horses always caught her attention, but the word iron puzzled her until she realized they were talking about a railroad being built between Sydney and Parramatta. Surprised that she hadn't heard more, she realized the reason she hadn't met these women before was because their husbands had been brought in to survey and prepare to build the tracks. Knowing that this could be a lucrative investment, she sought out her attorney who was not as forward thinking the next day.

"Mr. Saunders, it is my money and I have it to invest. I was asking you to find me those who are investing in the railroad so that I might buy shares. I was not asking your advice on how to spend my money. If this occurs again, I will seek out another solicitor for my business," she warned him, annoyed when he attempted to instruct her on how to invest and in what. He'd attempted to dismiss this investment, telling her it was a passing fancy and wouldn't pay a dividend. She knew differently, knowing people would move to Parramatta and the surrounding areas if transportation were easier. Not everyone had high-spirited horses to break in and work or business out there. People would want to live and invest in the area, and it would grow. It made her think more about the sawmill she had invested in and its possible

expansion. People would need lumber to build their homes and businesses.

"I assure you, Lady Worthington, I have your best interests at heart. I know you don't have a husband, and your sons aren't old enough to advise …" he began to bluster condescendingly, blinking rapidly at her threat to go elsewhere. They both knew speculation of why she had moved her business to someone else would ruin him.

"As you know," she continued as though he hadn't answered her, his stuttering response was annoying her further. "My friends are the owners of Lawrence and Twin Stations. I'm certain they can advise me not only on investments but on obtaining those who would work with me … instead of against me and my wishes."

"But if you had a man …" he began again, trying to be reasonable. This woman was most exasperating and if she'd only listen to him …

"My husband was a good man," she began angrily and was about to tell him off for bringing that up and decided not to antagonize him further. "He is gone now, God rest his soul," she added piously as she knew all good women should, even if she was relieved her husband was gone. "But he left me in charge of my sons' estates and money, and I will use it in a way that benefits us all."

"I was merely attempting to advise …"

"No sir, you were overstepping your place," she said with a steel tone. "I won't have it. In the future, if you want my business, you will remember this." She stared him down, gratified when he looked away first. She was about to start crying over this confrontation, but somehow, she remembered how Melissa would have handled things and it gave her strength. As it was, she was shaking and hid her gloved hands behind her reticule.

"Of course, my lady," he appeased her, nodding and bowing slightly. "I will have those names for you shortly."

"Thank you," she stated and stood up to leave. "I'll look for your missive." She left his office, thrilled that she wouldn't have to stay longer because she wasn't certain she could keep herself from crying in front of the man. If her father had been there, he would have talked all over her, and she wouldn't have stood a chance. After all, what could she, a mere woman, know about investments?

As she got in her coach, having chosen to use the large encumbrance for coming through town, she glanced at the guards, who were keeping the curious away. The large Worthington coat of arms were on each of the doors, and she wondered if coaches would go away some day. She preferred the carriage, but with the rains that might come in at any time, she had thought it advisable to use the larger vehicle. The men in the Worthington livery were an impressive sight. She thought musingly of what Melbourne's livery should look like someday.

Abigail was pleased to see a letter from Melissa in the mail that day. Although it read Mel Lawrence, she was one of the few who knew that Mel was actually Melissa. Her first love, she still thought fondly of her but was glad that she and her wife were doing so well out on Lawrence Station, where they lived with their children. In her letter, Melissa thanked Abigail for arranging with the governor to get the patents for their land. She'd been in correspondence with Carmen Pearson, the Hispanic woman from America lived on Twin Station and ran it with her cousin, they had also confirmed they had received the patents for their own lands. *Now, if we can just husband the land for the next generation, I know I will have succeeded in my reason for being here.*

The children need to be on their lands, and I'd like to educate them in both the White and the Aboriginal ways but keeping a teacher out here may prove to be difficult if they don't like the Outback. It isn't for everyone, she wrote.

Abigail put down the letter to think for a moment. Abigail smiled as she remembered teaching her own daughter her letters. While she wasn't certain their governesses could even read or write, she took pleasure in reading to her children nightly before they went to sleep. Agatha had pretended to read the same books when she looked at the pictures. Abigail would have to look into getting a tutor for her, but would the tutor be open-minded enough to teach a girl? Most would vie for the position if it was to teach her boys. After all, they were both lords, and her oldest son Augustus—named for her husband but called Auggie by the rest of them—would be going to England someday for his education. But what about Melbourne—whom she called Mel—her second son? She'd bought his title for him so that he too would be a lord, but he should be equally educated. She couldn't bear the thought of them both going back to England. Being separated from any of them for the length of their education was unthinkable to her. The fear of not knowing what could happen to them kept her on edge. What if their ship went down or her father got ahold of them? She tried not to worry about it too much because they were still little boys, but she did worry about their future. Why couldn't there be a school equally prestigious, here in Sydney?

The next chance Abigail had to associate with other women, she cut their gossiping short, having neither the patience nor the time for such. Usually, she steered their gossip to find nuggets of information she could use, but today she didn't have the tolerance. Instead, she

introduced the idea of establishing academies for the young men and women who had either been born here in Sydney, or who had emigrated with their parents for various reasons. "Not all can afford private tutors as I myself along with my brothers were accorded," she explained. "I was going to look for such here or send to England, but my dear friend Mel Lawrence mentioned her … um … his concern about their children and finding a teacher that would stay in the Outback on their station. I'm certain my friend Carmen Pearson will find the same problem on Twin Station." *There, that should get the ball rolling.* Even though it was her idea, she knew these women would discuss it with their husbands until one of the men came up with the idea for himself.

"Was your son Mel named for your friend that owns Lawrence Station?" one of the women asked innocently.

Briefly shocked, because that was exactly where the name had come from, she recovered quickly. She wanted no misunderstandings as to her son's parentage. She hid her anger behind a sugar-sweet smile. "Oh no, we named him after Lord Melbourne." She looked among the ladies who thought themselves her friends. "You know, the man that the city of Melbourne is named after?" At their accompanying and some knowing nods, she dropped her smile, and the women continued on with their incessant gossiping.

Abigail was not surprised to get a visit soon afterward from one of the ladies, asking if she would donate to an academy for young ladies and men.

"I would be thrilled to contribute, but I think it would be best if they were separate academies, one for the girls and one for the boys?" She knew that none of the men who had contributed to this idea would

approach her directly, relying on their wives to make the suggestion instead. It was the same type of business dealings she'd had to broker through her solicitor because men didn't do business with women, at least not directly.

It took months, years really, but eventually the Folsom Academy for young ladies was established and a woman who had run such in England was hired. Harbeaurt Academy for young men was also established and a headmaster installed who was from England but had also lived in America for a time, installed to run and administer it for the parents who had invested in these endeavors. In the meantime, Abigail was able to find a young man named Mr. Ford to tutor her children, with the hope to be hired at one of the academies later on. She had a maid stay with them at all times, not trusting anyone to be alone with her children. Mr. Ford was trustworthy, but she had heard of a tutor seducing their employer's child and she would take no chances. That salacious gossip must have influenced her decision. The door was to remain open; the children taught with both the tutor and a maid present. Occasionally, Abigail would pop in to see how her daughter was doing, and later, much later, her sons. Mr. Ford even agreed to move out to their home once it was built because the academies he would eventually apply for would be years in the making.

CHAPTER NINE

"Lady Worthington, I think I have found someone from amongst the men we hired who can supervise to finish the mill and houses we are building here in Parramatta," Shamus O'Grady told her when she came to inspect the work on the property months later. It had been raining hard for a month so the men were working inside, but the rain had stopped and they were rushing about outside, getting what they could done before another torrential downpour hit. It would be a brief reprieve as they were having one of the wettest rainy seasons that anyone could remember.

Abigail had fretted, knowing it was a terrible idea to ride out here with the bad weather, but it had been a while, and she was anxious to see the progress. The reports and missives she received were not enough to assuage her curiosity. She was wearing a slicker with a

sheepskin coat underneath, just like the ones she had seen Mel wear, to ward off the cold. Her men were similarly attired, and she could see by their expressions they hadn't appreciated the long ride in the miserable weather, but Abigail loved riding in the rain. She was careful to not let her hood fall down and expose her hair to it because a lady shouldn't enjoy it as much as she did.

"Does this mean you are ready to start on my house?" she asked, trying not to get excited. It was taking such a tremendous amount of time. She wanted to recommend Mr. O'Grady for the schools that were being discussed, but she also didn't want to lose him until her house and barns were built. She sat on her Thoroughbred, wondering if this would be the day when one of the horses stepped in a hole in the road and broke its leg. She'd been foolish to come out all this way with her expensive horse on a day like today.

"Aye, I believe me and my men," he thumb-pointed to a few of the men working around them, "are about done here and can start. They's," he then pointed to some of the ex-prisoners and other men, "can keep on with the work for ya."

"I would be ever so grateful," she confided. The time it had taken was really fraying her nerves, and while she had kept herself busy with other things, she really wanted to get her home built. She'd gone over the architectural plans many times since they'd been delivered months ago. The mill and workers' houses had been straightforward and redundant, but her home and barns were much more complicated. They'd outgrown the house in Sydney, especially with the dozen horses she had ordered from England. There simply wasn't as much room as these purebred and high-strung horses needed. Already she'd lost several grooms who couldn't keep up with their high spirits, and she'd

replaced them with men who assured her they had the wherewithal to cope with the fine beasts. She'd further complicated things with the young horses Mel had sent her, trading for a couple of the Thoroughbreds to interbreed them. Then she had purchased more horses from Carmen, bringing them from the Outback to breed with her fine stallion. Now they were more than maxed out for space in the stables.

"Ma'am, I ain't a horse trainer," Clarence had admitted. "I cans take care of them, clean up after them, rub 'em down, but I don't know nothin' about training 'em." He gestured at the overtaxed stable.

She agreed and had written Mr. Elmswood, explaining she wanted an up-and-coming trainer that he could recommend, hoping, he would have a man he had been training. A few of the grooms he had sent did not work out. Some had quit; others returned to England, not liking Australia and leaving all that had been familiar to them. But even those remaining were not up to training her expensive Thoroughbreds, much less breeding them. The added horses she had acquired only complicated those things.

Mr. Elmswood hadn't been thrilled to send the Thoroughbreds to Australia as she'd asked, but he had no choice but to obey her ladyship's request and send them on. She realized now that it had been too soon, and she would have been better off if she'd waited until the barns and paddocks were built on the land she had acquired.

"What shall you build first?" she asked, smiling at the Irishman. He had changed a lot since he had stopped drinking. He looked to have gained some weight and no longer had that white pallor that made him look ill.

"Well," he stated, putting his thumbs behind his suspenders as though considering. "I think we'll dig the cellars first," he said meaningfully. "If you're still wanting what we discussed?" There was enough innuendo in that statement that she knew what he meant. The drawings from the architect they had gone over had none of the secrets he intended to install. Having looked them over and been paid via the tax she'd given for the new buildings, the building commission had stamped their approval, and since she was a friend of the governor's, it had been expedited. The plans, though, had lain dormant while the buildings in Parramatta went up.

Abigail smiled, having been delighted at the sketches and ideas he came up with. While not masterpieces, her ideas were there on the papers, and he'd explained that he would call the tunnels drainage ditches, some of the hidden passages or rooms would be called closets, and only a few workers would really understand what they were for. "I do," she agreed with a nod. He'd shown her the final drawings, the official plans approved by the building commission, and then shown her where he'd be making alterations that wouldn't be known to too many others. In fact, they might not even realize they were secrets and forget about them after having built them. He'd made too many buildings in his day without the benefit of an architect, but, he supposed, a lady of the countess's stature had to go through official channels. He hoped that no one would ever find these things they'd be constructing or ask too many questions.

He smiled, having enjoyed sketching in the secret passages. He didn't understand why she felt the need to have them, dismissing it as something the gentry needed or wanted, but he would build it to her satisfaction. He'd already been approached by several men who

wanted him to build factories for them, but he'd had to turn them down, his commitment to the countess not over until he built her house and barns. He was loyal to her because she had given him this final chance. He'd known no other who would have gambled on him and his sobriety.

"Let's also start on one or two of the barns first," she suggested, knowing her stable in Sydney was filled to bursting and hoping to alleviate that.

"Before your house, m'lady?" he clarified, surprised.

"Yes. I'll be wanting the first barn for horses built, but later those for more horses and then sheep and other animals, but the house can be started after you've installed some of our secrets," she lowered her voice to indicate the tunnels and then continued, "and the other barns later."

Surprised at the order of things but hoping to keep her happy, he nodded. Already the second lumber mill was being built in a small village not far from the station she would be building, so he would have ready supplies of wood. The first mill owner sent his son to manage the second mill for her ladyship, and a nearby pond was being diverted for their use.

Abigail was unable to go out to the house site as often as she wished. The thirty-mile ride to Parramatta was bad enough, but a trip to the house, which was near the Blue Mountains, required at least an overnight stay. Those trips, though, she cherished. She brought

supplies in the wagons, making certain there were treats they couldn't have gotten or even thought of on their own.

She watched in wonder as O'Grady built the first of her grand barns for her charges. She'd chosen the Monitor style of barns, imitating Melissa's barns, but hers were larger and longer to accommodate far more horses. She had avoided the Gambrel style of barn, preferring the gables in the Monitor style and packing the upper levels with rich, dry hay from her own meadows. There was room in between each barn for a paddock to exercise the many horses she intended to have or to release horses from their stalls. Those first few cuttings were not good enough for her horses, and she sold the weed-filled bales to others, having the men that she had hired on to manage the farms pull up the weeds that were bad for their stock. She was having to learn from those in the know about the different grasses and plants that grew best here in Australia, that were bad for man or beast, and what they could do about that.

She had O'Grady build barracks with enough bunks to hold thirty groomsmen or more, with walls for privacy every four bunks. A large stove was in one corner so they could cook if they wanted, providing heat for the big barracks as well. A bathing room was attached, too—all the modern conveniences so they would be comfortable. Married farmers and groomsmen had bungalows made of a combination of the many rocks and cut lumber available to them. Each bungalow had one or two bedrooms, depending on their family's needs, but also a kitchen and a bathroom, something unheard of when so many had a dunny out back.

"I don't want to worry about sewage," she told her builder when she had explained this for the houses near the mill and continued on here on

the station. "Sometimes the wind blows nasty," she stated, wrinkling her nose.

Considering she worked with horses and their dung was useful on the fields, O'Grady thought it rich that human waste was where she drew the line. Still, he would make the countess happy, even if she was a little eccentric. "I'll have to send to England and America for some of the things you want in that house," he informed her, nodding towards the big house, enjoying the job and the rich woods she had insisted upon. Even the trees cut here in Australia, various kinds of eucalyptus and other species that he had been unfamiliar with until he used them, but staples like oaks and maples that Europeans had planted and other trees, were pretty. He loved the feel of them beneath his fingertips as he worked, some of the men who worked with him understanding the craftmanship. The beauty of this monument to the faith that Lady Worthington had in him and his building abilities was rewarded in the product he and his men had produced: the attractive home they were building for her. He took a lot of pride in the beautiful edifice that was being built. She hadn't wanted a castle or a uniform building like so many were building in Sydney. The architecture she had chosen was rich and elaborate but functional and perfect for this large station in the foothills. The views she would be accorded in the second and third stories and the cupolas in the corners of the house would more than justify the time and work they put into this edifice.

He watched as the other men she had hired put up boarded paddocks, the quality of the wood so much better than what they had produced in the saw pits since the wood mills had gone online. They'd been inundated with requests for this straight and solid wood that was produced, but they had to turn some people away because the wood

produced for the mill, houses, and station was a top priority. The mills were having a difficult time keeping up with those clamoring for the finer woods they were milling, no more were uneven and unaged woods being used in sawpits. Having quality wood available, even on a limited basis, was making the mills almost immediately turn a profit.

Abigail was thrilled when the first barn and paddocks were done so she could bring her babies out to the station. They had to be careful when letting the horses out into the vast fields so they wouldn't overeat the rich grasses. She loved seeing them able to gallop and play across the flats. Even watching the elegant horses graze in the vast fields was calming to her as she realized some of her dreams.

As they brought out some of her babies, one of the grooms was careless and a frightened young stallion pulled from his grasp. It ran off, galloping away as though the devil were on its heels with the groom in pursuit. Fortunately, a young woman from one of the smaller stations that lined the road caught the reins effortlessly, bringing the overheated young horse to a standstill and crooning to it as it foamed and breathed deeply. Willing to fight for its freedom until it heard her, his ears twitched and his eyes grew curious as to what she was saying. He calmed as she patted him.

Abigail could hear the groom berating the young woman for interfering by helping him. "How dare you touch him …" he was saying to hide his embarrassment.

"That will be enough of that," Abigail told him haughtily, stopping his diatribe as she rode up on her own mount, a fine Thoroughbred mare. "You, sir, should be more respectful to the lady." Although, it was obvious the unkempt woman was no lady, merely a commoner. "She kept you from losing your position," she said warningly, glaring

at the young man who had thought to take out his own frustration over losing the horse on the poor woman who had caught it for him.

His eyes widened at the tone her ladyship used, realizing the loss of this horse could have cost him his position. He bowed his head quickly and mumbled a hurried apology to the poorly dressed woman before leading off his charge.

"I am sorry for his behavior," began Abigail as she looked at the woman. She glanced about the yard, the poor state of the place giving her pause. She passed many small holdings on her trips out to Parramatta and beyond to the land she had purchased. She'd not given them or the people who occupied them a single thought. This one was poor, very poor, and she could tell the woman was embarrassed. "You easily caught my young horse," she said, keeping her voice even as she examined the woman while ignoring the state of her clothing, which was quite dirty.

"I knew horses growin' up," the woman admitted as a child came up to cling to her dirty skirts, his nose dripping and his face equally as dirty as their clothes. She looked alarmed at the guards who had immediately squared off around the lady.

"Oh? What kinds of horses?" Abigail found herself asking, wondering what impulse had her talking to someone who looked like this. She had met all kinds in her travels, but this level of poverty she had not encountered before. Then, she thought about that, she had seen poor people but had been raised to ignore them. She realized what a snob she had been. Even the Aboriginal villages she had encountered on her travels were in better shape than this unfortunate station, with its poor sheep and only a hovel to live in. Her heart went out to the woman she had started to converse with.

The woman stared at the well-dressed lady. She knew who she was, of course. She'd seen her riding those beautiful Thoroughbreds for a long time as she went to and fro about her business, her guards making certain she was well-protected. She'd stared longingly at the horses from afar, remembering better times, before … this. She looked about the unfortunate holdings her husband had been able to acquire for them, embarrassed to be seen looking like this. Her other dress she had washed just that morning. She realized she was keeping the lady waiting and answered quickly, "My uncle raised Yorkshire Coach Horses," she confessed, blushing as she looked at the fine bred Thoroughbred who stood so impatiently but was so expertly held by the woman. "I always thought it would be wonderful to raise Holsteins."

"The horse, not the cow I assume," Abigail found herself teasing. She smiled down at the woman who looked up suddenly and lost herself in the sad eyes before her. If Abigail found herself enchanted by the eyes, it was the smile that really threw her.

"Of course," she laughed, showing off a dimple. "But coachers were more practical to raise for money."

"Aye, they would be. I don't think anyone breeds them deliberately around here, though," she mused. She'd only seen farmers' horses. They weren't too discriminating in what they were breeding, needing strong-muscular horses for the farm work they would need them to do. She thought of the horses that Carmen was breeding, the two mares she now had. They would certainly do for coach work, and their offspring could …

"Well, there is nothing like these, though, either," the woman pointed out, the Thoroughbred nibbling at her sleeve for attention.

"Hey, come away there, you," Abigail said to her mount and startled the young woman who thought she was admonishing her for reaching out to pet her steed. "I thank you again for catching my young horse. I've enjoyed speaking with you,' she told her while turning her horse.

The woman watched longingly as the lady walked her horse away. She'd missed talking with others, her husband discouraging her from becoming too friendly with the neighbors. The few women she had met from the other small stations around them had been as bad or worse off than she. Some were slovenly, and a few were a bit slatternly. She didn't want that for herself or her children, and she cuddled her son closer from where he was hiding in her skirt before heading back to the hovel that was her house. She turned as the woman reached the road that led to Parramatta and waved, hoping to catch a glimpse of her again as she traveled between Sydney. It was one of the highlights of her dismal life here on their small farm, or station as they called it.

Abigail mused for a moment about the woman she had just met, wondering at her story. There were a lot of poor people trying to make a go at the raw, unkempt land that was Australia. She looked to the Blue Mountains, far off for now, and hoped that she wasn't making a mistake trying to build a stud out here where no one had succeeded before. Thinking about how poor the woman had looked and her surprise that the woman knew anything about horses, she thought about the woman's dark sad eyes and the delightful smile she had. She knew she'd been alone for far too long, longing for what she and Mel had had at one time and knowing it was up to her to find it again on her own. Or some semblance of it. She briefly wondered if the Sappho Club existed in Sydney and wondered how she would go about finding out.

CHAPTER TEN

At one of her tea parties, the countess overheard one of the ladies saying how unhappy their gardener was with tending their small townhome garden. Abigail sent Clarence around to steal the gardener for her estate, and the man had been ecstatic to be given basically carte blanche as he began to build her gardens around the house. While he had been alarmed at how far he was from Sydney, his enthusiasm grew at taming the raw lands around the house, sending away for European plants and talking to others who had lived in the area longer and knew plants he could substitute. He'd hired several young men to help him, a couple former prisoners who had the knowledge about gardening as her ladyship believed in giving them a second chance. She'd learned that some of the prisoners had misdemeanors that were innocent but found

guilty because more powerful people had their enemies shipped off with made up charges. While she wasn't foolish enough to believe any of their stories, she would employ those with the skills necessary on her new station and allow them the chance to start over. They could earn her trust unless they did something that warranted their dismissal. The new gardener of Brentford had been instructed not to dig down too far where the drains were, but other than that, he was creating beauty that Abigail and the children could eventually enjoy. It would take years for the plants, bushes, and trees he and his men planted to take hold and grow to their fullest, but in the meantime, he was planning, pruning, and experimenting.

"I don't know if I want a maze," she stated in answer to her new head gardener's exuberant question, remembering the estate gardens she had seen growing up. She particularly remembered Hedgerows, the estate her husband had kept her in. It was his family's estate, a virtual prison that she had hated. It would someday be Auggie's, but for now, her son was with her and would be raised on Brentford. She wondered if her daughter even remembered the estate she had been born on. She doubted it. Australia was all her children knew, although she kept the memories of England alive to them by telling them stories and describing what she had known and seen. She told them only positive, uplifting tales because she didn't want them to be fearful of her family or the things she herself had been through.

"I could make it a small one?" he pleaded, knowing mazes were all the rage on large estates back in England and he wanted to try it here. After all, they had plenty of room. "It will take years before it's tall enough …" he left off, not wanting to upset the countess while she contemplated these ideas. He'd been thrilled when she asked him to

make ponds, not only incorporating them in the various gardens with fountains and wildlife, but in the paddocks for the horses, a feat that had its challenges. He found they could make their own pipes, coating trees with clay and burning them in very hot fires. This way they could run the pipes they needed throughout the gardens and estate. For some reason the builder, that O'Grady gent wouldn't let him or his men dig in certain places.

"I don't want those trees taken down," she explained, not for the first time. She was unwilling to clear-cut areas and knew they would need plenty of shade for all the animals she intended to have on her station. Plus, some trees would be needed to hold back the waters that came down out of those mountains with the fall rains. Twice, new gardeners and fence builders had taken down trees she wanted left alone, which upset her greatly. Their positions in jeopardy, they were careful not to displease her ladyship or her plans for the station going forward. As a result, the gardeners knew that any trees that would be cut first they would have to have her permission and second would have to be on the further reaches of the station.

Abigail brought her children with her a couple of times to show them the barns where their horses were even now housed. All three of the children loved running about the grounds, watching as the men built more barns and their home. She had the governesses keep extra close eyes on the children since there were poisonous snakes and spiders out here. She loved picnicking with them under the trees, watching as the various birds native to Australia twittered in the trees.

"Mama, can I keep it?" Agatha asked when she found a kitten in the stables behind their home back in Sydney.

"Absolutely," she answered, noting Leesa Fredericks disapproved. "You will keep it in the stable and then make certain it's got a home in the barns when we move out to Brentford," she instructed the little girl. She could see the relief on the woman's face that at least the small animal wouldn't be in the house she was attempting to keep clean with the maids.

"I's heard that cats can smother small children," the woman explained later as they watched the little girl introduce the kitten to her pony.

"That's an old wives' tale," Abigail stated. "We will need cats—good cats—that can grow into good mousers to protect our barns out there." She nodded towards the Outback.

Abigail was looking forward to moving as soon as Mr. O'Grady said the house was ready. She was in love with the cupolas, dormers, and gables he had put up, some with the Worthington coat of arms visible. She must write to Sir Boardman and ask that a copy of the Brentford coat of arms be sent to her so she could have these made for the house and barns. It was only right that her second son have the same pride that Auggie would over being a lord of the realm. They both were lords in their own right, and she intended to instill that pride in the boys. They may be too young at present to appreciate it, but she knew how important their lordships and their estates would be someday.

Abigail had Clarence look out for any other cats and even dogs that they would need for Brentford Station. Eventually the estate name would be shortened to just Brentford, but for now, since a former station had sat on the property, they were calling it that. She'd hired a grazer to take a flock of imported sheep to graze down some of the

grasses that her horses would eventually be put on, not wanting any plants on there that could harm her babies. The grazer suggested goats for some of the weeds that the sheep and horses would not eat and to clear some of the land, especially under the trees she wanted to keep. He helped her find someone who was looking to graze their goats, providing milk that they could sell. The countess hired him and shared in the profit of the milk, cheese, and soap that his wife made. She provided them a cottage in exchange for their herd, clearing out fields that needed the animals. She cautioned about letting any get away as feral goats, she had heard, could be a menace. She also cautioned him against snakes since they both knew that goats were herbivores and wouldn't eat the snakes, but that poisonous snakes did exist in the Outback and could kill the animals and people.

Abigail was tired of the parties, picnics, and teas, where well-meaning friends were attempting to introduce her to young men who were suitable to someone of her station. As the Dowager Countess of Worthington, she was eminently superior to any and all they introduced her to. Trying to explain that her focus was on her children and their well-being didn't work as an excuse. She found that many men were willing to ignore her thoughts, feelings, and intelligence and instead looked to her fortune, her connections, and her status. This didn't appeal to her in the least, and while some might eventually become friends, others were ignored and avoided, much to their surprise. She

didn't appreciate arrogance, condescension, or the patriarchy that some exhibited.

She found herself wondering if she would ever meet someone appropriate, someone suitable and wondered at how Mel had met Alinta and they'd fallen in love. She still loved Mel, would always love her, but she'd resigned herself that theirs was just a friendship. It was built on the love they'd once had, but their opportunity had passed. Now she must find herself someone, and she knew it would not be a man. She didn't want a man to lord over her with his superior status just for being male. She loved her freedom. She loved her children. She was building her own home for her children's future. She didn't need a man. She wanted a woman, but how to find one that had the same tastes and interests. She'd speculated at the parties, picnics, and teas, and none were more than friends.

"What exactly are you looking for in a man?" one of the women ventured to ask when the prospect she had put forward had been rebuffed.

"I don't know really, but I know I won't allow him to be chosen for me as my father had with the late Lord Worthington, may he rest in peace," she stated piously, knowing that her behavior had to be above reproach. Already some had wondered at her building her station so far from Sydney, expressing concern about her being so isolated, but they didn't know how far it really was when they hadn't traveled much beyond the city.

"But Tommy Beauford had …" she began to defend her champion.

"A grown man going by Tommy and still living according to what his mother edicts was not what I was looking for," she tried to let her

friend down gently. She smiled to soften the blow. "And he doesn't even ride."

They all knew her horses; her Thoroughbreds were already generating talk because no one else had imported the lines she had. They didn't have access to such or have the money to indulge as she did. Several of the women nodded, agreeing with her about the horses. Anyone she got involved with would have to have more than a passing interest in horses. A couple of them understood about the prospect, though. Tommy Beuford was a mama's boy and far too old to do whatever the older woman said or dictated. Anyone taking on Tommy would have to take on his mother as well. They wouldn't, however, be bold enough to state it publicly as Lady Worthington had, even within their small circle. No one knew if they might need a favor and marrying such as Tommy might be necessary to a few of them.

"Why were you inquiring about work horses?" another ventured to ask, having overheard her conversation with one of the gentlemen.

"It was just a thought," she answered airily, as though she had a passing fancy. "After all, farmers and other station owners would need such. Not everyone can afford my beauties," she answered, referring to her Thoroughbreds. Everyone knew they were her babies and her main focus. They didn't realize that Abigail had many interests, and while she kept quiet at some of these social events, she also gleaned what information she could. It was how she had snatched up the gardener and heard of other farmers, grazers, and stockmen that she could send out to her station to work for her. She had even bought a couple of men's indentured servitude after her men had talked with them and found out if their skills matched what she needed on her station. She

also allowed the workers to send for their wives and children if they worked out and agreed to stay and work for her for a longer period.

"Would you breed them to your Thoroughbreds?" The woman obviously knew nothing about horses.

"Oh no, no, noooo," Abigail corrected her with a smile, not laughing at her. "This would be a separate venture." These people were so limited, keeping to the city and not seeing that Australia had so much to offer. She hoped that someday when she had her station up and running to her satisfaction, they would come and see that there was so much more than their small parties and soirees. She knew some of these women would be horrified to realize how far she really was from the center of their world. She didn't mind, and looked forward to the station she was building, slowly but surely.

"Aren't you afraid of traveling all that way into the Outback?" another inquired, not for the first time.

Abigail smiled. The Blue Mountains were not the Outback in her opinion. She'd been into the Outback by going to Lawrence and Twin Stations. If these women only knew how far away that really was, they would realize that the station she was building was merely a drop in the rain bucket in distance. She studied the woman for a moment, wondering if it was a genuine question or food for gossip later. She chose to believe it was the former and not the latter. "No, I'm not afraid in the least. I have my guards with me, after all, and my Thoroughbreds and other horses are bred for their endurance, not just their beauty." Abigail smiled; she could talk about her horses until she bored these ladies silly. She decided to educate them a little. "The horses seem to relish the trip," she said in a confiding voice and then added, "It's so beautiful out there, and in my opinion, that's not even

the true Outback yet until you get over the Blue Mountains. The station I'm building will someday be a destination and not just the home that I am building for my family."

She listened as the women chattered about how frightening it was to go beyond Sydney. They didn't seem to understand what freedom it gave the countess, and in their secular world, they were afraid to travel anywhere without a husband, son, or some male figure in their life escorting them.

"Might I have a word, Countess Worthington?" the reverend stopped her as she left church that following Sunday with her children, shepherding them before her.

Abigail looked up, surprised, and inwardly sighed, knowing where this might be going. "Of course," she stated, looking to her governesses to handle the children and get them in the coach. Already, her guards were standing by their horses awaiting her. Another that had escorted the family into church was standing a few feet away. Abigail stepped away from the path so the reverend could finish greeting his parishioners. This gave several people opportunities to stop and chat with her ladyship, whether she wanted to or not. Her thin, brittle smile was not noticed, but her impatience over having to wait for the conversation that the man wanted was becoming obvious by the time he had finished.

"Thank you so much, Your Ladyship, my apologies for keeping you waiting," he stated as he approached. He greeted others who had been

speaking with the countess and waited until they took the hint and left them alone.

"What can I do for you, Reverend Faulks?" she asked pleasantly, glancing to see the people gawking at the coach with the Worthington coat of arms on it, the guards in their uniformed livery, and the fine horses pulling it. She saw as Bonnie drew one of the boys back from leaning out a window and pulled the glass up so he couldn't do it again.

"I was wondering if the Worthington family would like to sponsor a pew?" he asked, coming straight to the point. He rubbed his hands together as though already having the money in hand.

"Sponsor a pew?" she asked, frowning.

He smiled smarmily; certain she was just hedging. "Ah yes, many of the families here in Sydney are sponsoring their pew so that their bench is always available to the family. It helps to raise money for our congregation," he explained.

She had heard nothing of the church raising funds this way and was certain the man had approached her first because of her money. He would then use her capitulation to his idea to solicit funds from other wealthy parishioners. This wasn't the conversation she thought he was going to start. She had thought one of the women had put a bee in his bonnet—so to speak—and brought her unmarried status to his attention. More than one man had mentioned that she should be married, but when she'd bluntly asked a few of them why, they could not answer. Stuttered replies about protection, companionship, and children didn't hold weight with her. She knew they meant control, advisement, and access to her money. She kept her smiles over that to herself. She knew that the Worthington money looked impressive, and it didn't hurt her cause to have the coach to avail herself of. She

glanced at it again and could see that Agatha was now pressing her nose against the window to see where her mother was at. She frowned at the girl and saw someone pull her back. "Reverend Faulks, we will be moving out to our estate—I hope soon. Then a reserved seat in your church would become useless to us," she explained, trying to word it delicately. She knew the offerings that she put into the church basket every week were probably not enough for this greedy and ambitious man.

"You've been building for quite some time. Have you thought of putting up a church for your people in a nearby village or perhaps on the estate?" he asked. He was already thinking of someone he could recommend for the pulpit for her ladyship. It would be a feather in his cap to have someone owe him such a favor.

She hadn't, but she smiled. "I'll speak with my builder when next I see him," she answered diplomatically.

"Mrs. Franklin mentioned that you were seeing Tommy Beauford?" he asked next.

"No, I am not seeing him. He was put forth as a possible candidate for my hand, but really, we are not compatible." Inside, she was angry at Mrs. Franklin for even mentioning it to the reverend.

"Well, he is a fine catch …" the man began, championing the man's best traits.

Abigail was tired of this conversation and interrupted to ask, "And I suppose he would bring his mother to live with us, were we to marry?"

The reverend blinked, surprised not only at her interruption but also at her question. "Well, of course. He does support her, after all. Surely you would welcome her …"

"No sir. You see, after being married to Lord Worthington, God rest his soul," she said, sounding pious, and not for the first time, "I find that I have to be careful who I might spend the rest of my life with. My sons are young and vulnerable, as is my daughter. It is my duty to see that their wealth is intact for when they marry and start lives of their own." He was nodding, smiling, and agreeing with her. "So you see, dear Reverend Faulks, that me marrying has to take careful consideration of all these factors, and taking care of a man's mother, when I have three little ones of my own, simply is too much to ask of me." She smiled in return. "Good day, Reverend," she said as she took the opportunity to leave his obnoxious presence and head for her coach, with her guard following a few steps behind. The footman saw her coming and held the door as she climbed the steps to sit inside.

The reverend, used to women agreeing with everything he suggested, had found himself agreeing with her ladyship instead. The countess was a very wealthy widow, and of course, she had the two lordships and her ladyship to raise in a proper household. He could see where marrying someone like Tommy Beauford would not be compatible with her plans for her offspring. It did not stop him from considering other men for her hand in marriage. After all, a respectable and wealthy widow such as herself needed the strong hand of man who could control not only her but the wealth he imagined she had access to.

CHAPTER ELEVEN

"Governor, might I have a word?" Abigail asked sweetly, meeting him at the Forrester's ball. She was dressed in a lovely cerulean-blue gown of the latest style, her hair done up on her head with ringlets hanging down. She looked quite becoming.

"May I have this dance?" he asked in return, bowing to her politely and silently wondering what else she would ask of him. He'd been quite generous, he felt, and he hoped she wouldn't want something he couldn't provide. His wife was a great admirer of hers, appreciating her insight into her dressmaker, styles, and social things that the woman hadn't understood before and he appreciated her ladyships friendship. Knowing the countess, his wife had risen in the rather limited social circle of Sydney.

As they danced, she asked casually, "Do you know a Major Banks?" She saw him shake his head. "Of her Majesty's cavalry?" she

confirmed. He again shook his head. "I believe I met him before he went out into the Outback this last time. He's been out there a few times," she explained.

"Are you interested in this man?" he asked, smiling, certain she was inquiring to see if he was worthy of her hand. If this was the case, his wife would want to know immediately. Speculation as to whom the countess was seeing, who was courting her, and who she would finally decide upon was running rampant. All the ladies were atwitter, according to his wife.

She shook her head, smiling, but inside she was fuming. The letter from Carmen with a copy of her journal, telling of the highhandedness of this major was infuriating. She switched tactics, confusing the governor for a moment. "You remember my friends from Twin Station that you so generously had their station surveyed so they could get ownership?"

"Ah yes, that name I do recall. Carmen Pearson and Fabiola Polaski was that the names?" he asked, wracking his brains. He met so many people in his duties as governor. "An American and a Polish woman?" he said musingly. He had an eye on the unusual or unique situations that he'd come upon in his colony.

"Well, Carmen is from California … America," she confirmed. "She's of Spanish and Mexican descent on her mother's side, but her father was American." She smiled as he grinned, pleased that he had remembered previous conversations. "Fabiola, though, is of Aboriginal and English descent, born right here in Australia on her father's station." She could see he was of the mind that there should be no mixings of the blood, as several English felt, but she kept her face impassive as she continued. "She and Carmen as well as Fabiola's

brother inherited the station together, and after her brother Harold's death, the two are running the entire station themselves."

"Do they need help? Two women alone …" he offered, puffing up with male pride and dominance as though he would be the hero to these two poor women. Alone in the Outback they would obviously need male guidance now that the brother was gone.

"Oh no," she said, shaking her head, the curls that Brodie had put into her hair bobbing becomingly under the chandelier, the lights shining off the blonde brilliance, catching several men's eyes at the attractive combination. "Two more competent ranchers, or grazers as you call them here in Australia," she chuckled self-deprecatingly "you could not have. Why, if Fabiola was born part sheep, I wouldn't be surprised," she teased, earning a delighted outright laugh from the governor. Several people turned as they danced by, wondering at his laughter and what the countess could be saying to amuse the normally reserved man.

"This sounds like women I would like to meet," he answered charmingly, turning her in time with the music on the dance floor. He knew he was the envy of several men who would give their eyeteeth not only to meet the countess, but to have her obvious wealth and her person all to themselves, if only for a dance.

"They are delightful women," she agreed, fanning his male ego a little. "Did you get their letter?" she asked innocently, holding her breath.

"Their thank you card?" he asked, nodding, certain this was why she had asked for a word. She was the epitome of good manners, and he'd encouraged his wife, who raved about her, to emulate her good behavior.

"Well, I know you got *that*," she said, smiling, but inside she was irked. She was certain the letter she was speaking of had been waylaid by one of his secretaries. The contents in it were quite alarming. In fact, from the nearly identical letter Carmen had written to her, she became incensed at the high-handedness of this major and the difficulties he had caused the two women, who happened to be her friends. "But no, I was talking of the difficulties that Carmen and Fabiola had with this Major Banks?" She was still being pleasant, but inside she was seething. She knew the man had probably thought two women alone had no power, but he would soon learn that the women had friends—powerful friends. She wondered if Carmen had written Mel because Mel too would be incensed at what had happened to her friends.

"Difficulties?" He shook his head. "I know of no difficulties. What are you talking about?"

"Oh dear," she said, biting her lip becomingly, attempting to sound innocent. "I may have been sticking my nose in where it doesn't belong." She sounded sincere, and her violet eyes opened wide.

"My dear lady, what *are* you talking about?"

"I'm sorry, Governor, but I know Carmen and Fabiola wrote you about this, and I thought you knew. I had hoped you would have made a decision about the situation, and before your official letter reached them, I could write to reassure them."

"I'm sorry, Lady Worthington, but I have absolutely no idea what you are talking about?" He looked intrigued, which was what she was counting on.

"Rather than get this second hand from me, I would like you to read the letter I received from them? Is it possible that you and your wife

could come to lunch tomorrow? If you're not too busy?" She knew, the governor's time was quite valuable and that he was always busy, but by inviting his wife, perhaps she could get him to come as well.

"I'll have to check my calendar …" he began musingly, trying to think what was on it. He'd only come to this ball tonight because his wife kept track of their personal itinerary. His duties as the governor were kept track of by his secretary.

"I would appreciate it," she assured him as they completed the dance.

He bowed to her. "I will get back with you and …"

"Thomas, what in the world was Lady Worthington telling you? I could hear your laughter from across the room?" Maisy asked her husband with a smile, pleased that he had danced with her ladyship, giving her something to brag about when she gossiped with her friends.

"I was just inviting the two of you to lunch tomorrow if you're available." Abigail put in before the governor could answer. "He was telling me he must check his calendar."

"Oh, Robert, I would like it if we could go," she said, clapping her hands together like a child about to get a treat.

"My cook has learned how to make those meringues you love so, Maisy," Abigail added with a smile, hoping Mrs. Harris had the fixings because she'd be asking her to make them if they came to lunch.

"I'll send a missive as soon as I've checked with my secretary," he promised, inwardly smiling at how easily her ladyship got her way with all of them. He didn't mind; her charm was only one of the many reasons they all enjoyed her company.

"Thank you so much for inviting us," Maisy answered, reaching out to squeeze the countess's arm so any who might be watching—and there was always someone watching—could see.

"This is very serious," the governor stated after reading the letter and the copied journal. It had taken him some time as he read and reread some of the passages. "I will take this up with his superior officers immediately. I can't believe the cheek of this man!"

Abigail stayed calm, but her heart was beating hard in her chest. She didn't want to overplay her hand, but she also didn't want Carmen arrested by the major. The fact that the Hispanic American woman had left the soldiers afoot would not go over well with the prideful English officers, much less the enlisted men. It could have been a death sentence, but fortunately, she had left their supplies for them further on down the track. That officer had no authority to be searching her men or allowing his men to harass her employees. His arrogance at attempting to take over on the two women's station as well as his soldiers behavior was something to read.

"I am sorry to be the bearer of bad news, but as you well know," she gestured towards the papers the governor had just read, "one bad apple can spoil the whole bin. It sounded like his men were taking their cues from him."

He nodded musingly as he reread parts of the missive again to memorize them. "And she sent the same to me?" he said. He shook his

head angrily. He would bet one of his secretaries was friends with this Major Burns or owed him a favor. He would find out who!

"Thomas, let's not ruin our luncheon with the countess?" Maisy put in cleverly, bringing him back to the present and away from his duties as governor.

"He hasn't ruined it. I fear by bringing this situation to his attention that I have ruined our lunch," Abigail returned, indicating the letter he was even now refolding to put in his suit pocket.

"I may keep this?" he asked before tucking it away at her nod. "You can write Mrs. Pearson and Miss Polaski that I am aware of the situation and will get to the bottom of this. Major Banks will have his day of reckoning, I assure you." His voice was raised in anger.

"Thomas, you are not giving a speech, and we do have our lunch to get to here," Maisy reminded him.

"Of course, my dear, of course," he answered, patting her hand.

The servants began to bring in the first course of their lunch at Abigail's signal. She had waited until she was certain the governor was on Carmen and Fabiola's side and had read the letter completely. Now, it was all up to him.

"And you say you may be moving soon to your station, even though it isn't finished?" Maisy was asking after they had been eating a while and had discussed everything except the incident that Abigail had brought up first and foremost to be addressed.

"Well, my builder, Mr. O'Grady, has enough of the house finished that we can live there. It isn't completely finished as I said," she confirmed. Talk of this luncheon would surely make Maisy the center of attention when she next met with the gossipy women.. "So, I won't have my ball yet, but when it is, you will be the first couple I invite.

Remember, it will take you quite some time to get out there and I do have rooms to accommodate you, so I'm thinking a weekend with picnics and shooting and riding. Maybe a full week," she added as though she had just thought of it.

"Oh, it sounds quite lovely," Maisy answered, accompanied by her familiar clapping of hands, which was so childishly endearing. "A country party!" She'd never attended one of those back in England; her husband hadn't been important enough then. But now she would be thrilled to be invited to Her Ladyship's event. The prestige alone would be enough to carry her for a long time as she regaled those who wouldn't be invited.

"Exactly," Abigail confirmed.

CHAPTER TWELVE

It was well over two years after she had hired O'Grady when he finally gave her the word that she could move into her unfinished mansion in the foothills of the Blue Mountains. While not complete to his satisfaction, it was near enough that he wanted her living there so she could have he and his men change anything that wasn't up to her liking.

She'd already hinted at him building additional houses in Parramatta for the mill workers and a second mill as the businesses grew. Mr. Evans had stated they could use the additional space because their mill was already up and running and handling small stations crops, and he could see the potential. Other investors such as the MacArthurs and the Marsdens had also begun to build their own mills to handle the enormous amount of wool that came from the Australian interior.

Abigail had asked to purchase Mel's next crop of wool, writing and explaining about the mill she had built. She wasn't certain they could handle Twin Station too. Evans was getting the hang of processing the wool with the latest machines they had imported from England. He'd trained men and women in the colony who were seeking employment. She was anxious to see that they serviced as many of the stations as they could. Having a second mill started would ensure their capabilities as they continued to grow.

She'd had a tentative thought about building a dye plant too, having written Mr. Cherwin about that very thing and the men they would need to run it. He'd expressed concern over losing the lucrative wool from Australia to their competing with their own mills in England, but she assured him there was room for both. She wrote about how fast Australia was growing and that there would a need for both. She also suggested he look into the possibility of expanding into the Americas as well, something Mel had suggested. She trusted Mel and her insight into business. Mel's father had taught the woman very well, and Abigail remembered the man fondly because of their shared love of horses. The countess now owned many of the horses the man himself had purchased. Anything regarding America, she felt Mel, who had been born there, must be an expert on.

"Ma'am, I don't wish to go to the Outback," Bonnie confided as they packed up their household, the landlord being informed that after all these years they were vacating the premises.

"Oh, Bonnie, you've been with us for so long taking care of the children," she lamented. "Isn't there anything I could say to entice you to change your mind?" she asked, genuinely concerned for the woman.

"I met a young gentleman and we've been stepping out. When I says that we were going to move out there," she gestured inland towards Brentford, down Parramatta Road and past the settlement it was named for. "He says he can't live without me and woulds I marry 'im?"

"You're going to be married?" she asked, surprised and pleased and disappointed all at the same time. At the woman's nod she smiled and wished her congratulations even though she didn't completely mean it. Abigail would be sad to lose this valuable maid. She briefly thought back to the days in England, where the maid would have asked her permission before accepting such a proposal, but she tamped those thoughts down. Australia was a new place, and while the rules should still apply, she wasn't going to be like those nobles who felt they owned those who served them. The woman was a paid servant, not a slave.

"Thank you, ma'am," she said, bobbing a curtsy. "I am very grateful for the job you gave me, but I's be wantin' me own children someday."

"Of course you do, and if you ever need a letter from me for another position, you let me know and I'll write a good one for you! Or, if you need a job, I'd welcome you back!"

"Well, the position of Mrs. is good enough for me for now," she answered cheekily.

Abigail was at a loss, having to find another governess to watch her children. Not many wanted to go beyond the city and while Sydney

was growing, so was Parramatta. The station though was a ways out and as she thought about Twin and Lawrence Stations, she knew she'd have a hard time finding someone who would be willing to go out into that wilderness, even if the Blue Mountains were only a mere couple of days from the large city. She thought about the train that even now tracks were being laid for between Sydney and Parramatta, that would change the amount of time it took to get places, and the people who would now move into the Parramatta area. That didn't help her now as she attempted to replace the valuable servant. One governess for three children wouldn't be fair and she hoped the other maids would help in the meantime.

They were also going to need more men. Even the farmers and herdsmen she had hired had needed incentive to work out on the remote Brentford Station. She'd sent her head gardener out to the MacArthur estate to get an idea of what she expected, informing him that she wanted some of the same things on her own property but not a copy of their gardens. Brentford would be unique, but she needed people to help her achieve her dream. She needed knowledgeable people to do great work to advise her along the way.

CHAPTER THIRTEEN

Abigail was thrilled to finally move to her estate. She would eventually throw a party to invite her friends from Sydney, but she wanted to give the property time to heal and establish its beauty. She was pleased that O'Grady had left a few of the huge eucalyptus trees near the house for shade, and her gardener had planted other trees that would eventually bloom, providing her with the beauty she sought. There were also attractive groves contained in the various paddocks to offer shade for the many horses she hoped to raise here in Australia. She'd had a track built beyond the various barns and paddocks, enclosed so the horses could be trained for racing if she so desired and exercised if she didn't. Already the hedges for the courses were growing in, and she looked forward to riding her horses on those courses.

She realized her gardens would never be as beautiful as the MacArthur's, but the gardeners she had hired would make the place uniquely their own. Nothing like the Worthington estate, Hedgerows. That had been her plan all along: to make her second son's inheritance an estate of exceptional and distinctive flare. She had it made known it was named: Brentford and not something like Hedgerows South or just another Hedgerows. This was her son Mel's estate, not an extension of what was back in England and her Auggie's inheritance. As she had watched the addition of fountains, flowers, bushes, and even trees, she looked forward to their growth filling in the scars on the land from the construction. The difference in buildings, the land, the plants, and even the grasses made it distinctive.

One need she hadn't anticipated was the number of wagons she would need to transport all her help and move all the items from town out to the new place. Fortunately, Clarence and Mr. Evans had thought of it and arranged for enough wagons to move the entire household.

As they passed through Parramatta, she waved to the people at the smaller stations, ones she had passed by over the past years but rarely interacted with other than a nod or a smile from horseback. She knew from gossip that they knew who she was and that her station was out beyond the village, quite a way beyond but still out here.

As they went through one of the smaller villages, she was alarmed to see a man beating an Aboriginal woman, another White woman attempting to stop him.

"You there, you stop right now," she ordered, as two of her guards got down and held the man back from striking the woman again. "What is going on here?" she demanded.

"That's me wife!" he shouted, lunging against the burly guards' hold. Her men stood there impassively, awaiting her ladyship's command.

Another of the guards came up. "M'lady?" he asked and she looked to see her captain of the guard.

"Fetch the magistrate, Phillips!" she ordered, getting down and approaching the women. "Are you okay?" she asked the Aboriginal woman, but she stared blankly ahead, seeming to accept her fate regardless of what it would be. She turned to the White woman, startled to recognize her as the woman she had met so long ago with the horses. "You!" she said. "Are you alright?" Having only met her when she was on her horses in the past, she was surprised to see she was of similar height. Seeing her up close, and this time at least clean, she noticed other things about the woman. Today the woman was wearing a clean frock, not very attractive but at least not full of dirt.

"I am, m'lady," she said, attempting to curtsy but doing a bad job of it.

Abigail nearly smiled at her attempt. "Do you know what's going on here?"

The man was shouting, "That's me wife! You don't have the right …"

Abigail turned back at the interruption. "Shut him up," she ordered her men, and one of them took a clean handkerchief from his pocket and stuffed it in the man's mouth before grabbing his arm again before he could remove it. The man was struggling hard. She turned back to the White woman and repeated, "Do you know what's going on here?"

The Aboriginal woman's dress was torn, revealing part of her back, which was crisscrossed with scars. Abigail was familiar with those

marks, having seen a horse whipped to this point before. While the scars looked different from a horse on the woman, she could tell they had been made by a whip. But the man had been beating her with his fists.

"No, I don't, m'lady. I was at the market," she nodded towards the village, "when's I saw thems and what 'e was doin' to 'er."

"You were right to intervene. No one deserves that." She nodded towards the mute woman. "Where are your children?" she asked, looking around.

"They's here," she said, gesturing to two children. One, a toddler, came out from under a table where he and his sister had been hiding when their mother entered the fray. The older one, a girl, asked, "Are you all right Mama?"

"I am, Natasha. Don't you fret," she reassured her, picking up the toddler, who stuck his thumb in his mouth and blinked at the countess.

"This is a new one, isn't it?" Abigail asked her.

"Aye, I had a second one since we last spoke, m'lady. This is Bradley, named after me husband."

"I'm sorry, I don't know your name. We never got around to introducing ourselves …"

"Everyone knows who you be, m'lady. The Countess of Worthington is well known on this road." She laughed. "I'm Merilynn. Merilynn Sorkin."

Abigail supposed everyone had seen her comings and goings\. "Well, Mrs. Sorkin, I am most pleased to make your acquaintance," she said sincerely. They both turned as the struggling man started choking on the handkerchief, trying to say something. "You may wish to make certain he doesn't swallow your kerchief," Abigail said dryly to her

guard, nearly laughing over her witty statement. The guard checked and then pushed even more of the material in the man's mouth. "Do you know who this is?" she asked, indicating the man and the Aboriginal woman.

"I've seen them around, but no, I've never made their acquaintance," she confessed as she shook her head.

They stood there until a rather paunchy man came running up with her captain of the guard. "M'lady, are you okay?" he asked, out of breath as he removed his hat and tried to bow at the same time, nearly bowling himself over at her feet.

Abigail looked on, amused, but hid it quickly as the man straightened up. "Are you the magistrate here?" she asked imperiously.

"I am, ma'am. Randolph Tierney at your service, m'lady," he stated, attempting to remove his hat that was already in his hands, flustered at talking to a lady of the realm. He knew who she was; he'd seen her riding past on her fine horses for years.

"We came upon this man beating this woman. He claims to be her husband," she stated, pointing to the couple and then making a gesture to have her guard remove the handkerchief.

The man swallowed a couple of times before stating, "That's me wife!"

"So you have said," the countess interjected, not giving anyone else a chance. "Do you have proof of that?"

The man looked surprised to be addressed by her, as well as by her lofty tones. He blinked a couple of times, glancing around at the men and particularly at the two holding him back. He tried repeatedly to get his arms free, but the guards held fast, looking to the lady dressed in fine clothes for orders to release him. She shook her head. "She's my

wife," he stated again, attempting to speak correctly. "We's been together for years now."

"Were you married in the church?" she asked quietly.

"I'll take this, m'lady," Randolph Tierney attempted to assert his authority.

"I would like an answer to my question," she said instead, turning towards the magistrate.

Realizing the countess held sway here and could create a lot of problems for him, he backed down. "You heard her, answer the lady," Tierney said, trying to save face.

The man looked ashamed. "No, I didn't marry her in the church. She's me common-law wife."

Although Abigail didn't quite know how Mel had met her wife, she had heard whispers about Alinta from some of the women on the station. She could only imagine how this man had obtained this woman as his 'wife.' "I would suggest that she come with me until you figure out if they are legally married," she said to the magistrate.

"Come with you?" he asked, surprised that a lady of the realm would get involved matters such as this. He knew the man, knew he drank, and his beating of his wife was his business. However, if they weren't really married …

"Yes, I believe she might not want to be his wife and would certainly be better off away from this …" she looked the man up and down as though she had stepped in something she shouldn't have, her nose wrinkling as if she had smelled something unpleasant. "… man."

"M'lady, please," her captain of the guard stated, attempting to keep her from embarrassing herself.

Abigail sent a warning glance to the man before turning back to her audience. While the man continued to struggle with her guards, she approached the woman. "Excuse me, do you speak English?" she asked kindly. The woman never looked around, still in the trance, accepting whatever fate these White people wanted for her. Abigail looked up and around to see her wagons had stopped and everyone in her household was watching. She signaled to Mrs. Fredericks and watched as she climbed down slowly from the wagon seat she had been sitting on.

"Could you help her into the wagon and see that she gets cleaned up when we get to the station?" she asked. She was astonished as the Mrs. Fredericks shook her head but complied against her own wishes. She hesitated to touch the Black woman, but with a flick of her head, the new maid, Moll, jumped from the wagon to help her. Between the two of them, they got the Aboriginal woman into the back of the wagon, and Moll sat with her, while a clearly disapproving Mrs. Fredericks pulled herself back up to her seat.

"You can't take me wife!" the man called, still struggling against the guards holds on him.

"Please take this man to your jail until such time as you have determined if he really is married to her," Abigail nodded towards the woman in the back of the wagon. "I would like to file charges for his beating of her."

"Ma'am?" her captain of the guard asked, astonished.

"I … well … I … don't know," the magistrate admitted, unsure about this situation.

"If you find that he is indeed married to her, he can claim her at my station. If not, I expect to find that my charges have merit and that he

will suffer the consequences of his actions." she continued. "You can contact my solicitor. Or perhaps I should take this up with my friend, the governor?"

The man's eyes nearly popped out of his head at her so casually dropping that she knew the governor. He also knew it wasn't worth his job to disagree with this lady. He would certainly try to do as she asked. "Could your men help me get him to jail?" he asked instead.

She nodded and the larger guards immediately began to march the abusive man to the village. They kept his arms up so it hurt to go down, he had to tiptoe to keep up. The magistrate hurried ahead to open the door ahead of them. She watched, looking at the crowd that had gathered. She turned back to Merilynn.

"Thank you so much for attempting to stop him." She nodded towards the Aboriginal woman. She looked nothing like her friend Alinta, but then, she supposed, they were of different tribes. "We'll take care of her."

Merilynn nodded, stunned at how her ladyship had taken control of the situation. Everyone had obeyed her instantly. She found it intriguing that this woman, a *mere* woman, had so much power over men.

"I'm so happy to have met you again, Mrs. Sorkin," she stated, holding out her gloved hand.

"Please, call me Merilynn," she returned. She let go of her little girl's hand to curtsy awkwardly and shake Abigail's hand, even as she held onto the toddler Bradley and her basket, which dangled precariously.

"Careful there," Abigail told her, catching the basket after letting go of the brief handshake. "I'm the Countess of Worthington, Lady

Worthington," she told the woman with a smile, her violet eyes twinkling at the woman. "I'll look for you when I travel here. Are you still on your station?" She gestured down the road.

"I am," she admitted wanting to laugh, as if she didn't know who the lady was. She didn't want the woman to come to her poor holding. The place was in even worse condition than it had been the last time she'd stopped. The sheep had grazed it down to nothing. And with the drought this section of Australia was experiencing, all the stations in the area were worse for wear.

"Well, as you can see," she gestured to the line of wagons and horses, "we are moving house. I won't be here as much, but I do have business in Parramatta, so I hope to see you."

Merilynn recognized a dismissal when she heard one, and bobbing another curtsy, backed up as one of the guards brought her ladyship's horse up. Using his cupped hand, Abigail got into the saddle easily, holding the reins as though she were born to it. Merilynn was astonished to see her ladyship rode astride her horse, her skirts splitting and cleverly hiding the fact.

Abigail looked down at the woman and nodded, indicating to those driving the wagons to get going as they waited for the two guards who had escorted the man to jail. As the wagon went by, the Aborigine woman still sat as if in a trance, despite Moll attempting to engage her in talk. Once the two guards returned and mounted up, they boxed Abigail in and went to catch up with their wagons, easily doing so with her Thoroughbred and their Brumby mixes.

Merilynn watched from where she stood after walking away, unaware that she was staring until Natasha commanded her attention. As they walked slowly back to their small station, she wondered what

Brentford, the station the countess owned, was like. She'd heard the gossip about the eccentric woman and certainly seen the comings and goings of the many wagons, men, and supplies that went up the road these past years. She'd admired the fine horses she'd seen the woman and her men riding and dreamed of the days on her uncle's farm and the horses she took care of there.

CHAPTER FOURTEEN

They took the road that would lead them along the Blue Mountains, the ridges standing prominently above the flatlands that held groves of trees and wide-open land that she enjoyed. The suppliers and builders having carved out this road and it stood as if it had always been there in this timeless land. As they came to the entrance of Brentford, she was pleased with the wrought iron gates that had finally been installed. Going up fifteen feet, they spread out as if angel wings to the brick columns, where the hinges allowed them to swing wide. The gatekeeper lifted his hat as her ladyship and her children passed by. She stopped to admire them as she looked up and down the line. The wrought iron extended on each side with ten-foot sections between columns every fifty feet before continuing transitioning to wooden fencing. The wood was milled in her own mill, the wood consistent

from the saws instead of the variations in size and quality that could be found from a sawpit. Each board was four inches across, three quarters thick, and one foot from the other. She'd had them put up so they were five feet high, a height that few horses would jump, although, her Thoroughbreds could if she trained them. Some would try, regardless of the height she made them. She'd had these painted black to match the wrought iron. Already, the gardeners were training flowers she didn't know the name of to climb along the posts and brick and then onto the slats and wrought iron of these beautiful fences.

"Lady Worthington, I'd like to show you …" was a common phrase O'Grady started with as he showed her all the secret places in her new home. Her various trips while the buildings took shape helped her stay on top of changes she wished him to make. No changes were shown on the drawings he'd had made up for the building committee, modifying the architect's original works in secret. She'd loved every passage, every staircase, and the tunnels from the house to the primary barns. She'd clapped with glee at the secrets, enjoying his sparkling eyes as they twinkled with their shared conspiracy. "I have to tell you; there were times I had to build some of this meself if I couldn't think up a good reason for the extra work to my workers." He laughed because the tunnels between the house and barns, one of the first things he had built from the cellars which even now were filling with fine wines that the countess was acquiring. He had called them drains as he and several bricklayers had put them in.

"Oh, I almost don't want you to ever be done," she'd told him ingeniously, relishing the secrets and the joy of having all of this finished, although there was still a lot to do.

"Well, some of this will takes some more time," he admitted, having kept additional men that he needed in order to finish the work faster. Since some of the men were prisoners, they'd had no choice, but many of them had been free workers and he'd had them start their work on other buildings on the property in order to ensure the pace of work continued. Now she wanted another mill and added houses built back in Parramatta and he was glad so that he wouldn't lose such good workers. He'd weeded out a few of the bad ones, and those whose sentences were up were offered positions if they wanted. He'd paid fair wages, and many had stayed on. The size of his crews was more than double what he'd had in the past when he worked in the Outback for her friends.

"Have we moved in too soon?" she fretted, looking about as the men brought in the furnishings she had sent for, had built, or had found on shopping expeditions with some of the ladies in Sydney. Some of her Sydney friends had enjoyed taking her to places they knew or discovering them with her. The excited giggles and chattering had worn on her nerves, but their advice and enthusiasm had been invaluable.

"Nay, my lady. You'll just have to listen to some banging on a bit as they finish over the coming months. I thought you was anxious to be here …?" he worried. He could smell the paint from one of the wings of the house.

"I have been, and I spent more time on that road than I cared to," she admitted. But it hadn't been all bad. The Thoroughbreds had needed their exercise, and she often brought a second horse with her to ride on the return trip. A sixty-mile ride, while excessive to a lady of her position, was manageable once or twice a week. She knew some of

her guards hadn't appreciated what a ride like that did to their backsides, and she'd heard the complaints. Still, she looked about the house which she loved, across the extensive gardens that led up to the barns that held her babies and thought it would be an excellent place for her children to grow up.

"Mama, my pony can't be in the main barn?" Agatha asked, coming in and looking as though she were about to cry.

"Who says so?" she asked, distracted as Mr. O'Grady touched his cap respectfully and went back to work.

"Mr. Perry says that the main barn is for your Thoroughbreds and the breeding program. What's a breeding program?" the little girl asked curiously..

"It's where we decide which horses are allowed to have babies and who the daddy will be," she simplified, annoyed with the man. He had come all the way from England with more horses for her stud. How dare he tell little Lady Worthington where her pony could be kept? She glanced to where Brodie had her hands full with the twins. The boys were more than toddlers now and always going in opposite directions. Abigail had offered to have Mrs. Fredericks help her maid, but the woman had been promoted officially to housekeeper and had her duties too. She glanced to where Mrs. Fredericks' son Joseph was with the twins. He was their best friend, a companion, and the pot boy for the house. She knew the boy had been raised in her own nursery, but as he wasn't a son of the house, she'd had to make him useful and started him as a pot boy. Now, when he wasn't working, he still played with the boys, causing as much mischief as they. She turned back to her daughter, considering the pony situation. The boys would be getting their own ponies soon, but she wanted to wait until the chaos of the

move was over. She wasn't about to tell the girl more about the breeding program.

She turned to her butler. "Mr. Jefferies, can you and your missus supervise the rest of the move in?" she asked him. She knew he was upset that his wife hadn't automatically been given the housekeeper position, but Mrs. Fredericks had been with her household longer.

"Of course, my lady," he said, bowing to her and thinking it was his duty after all. She wasn't necessary to him getting the servants to bring things in from the wagons. Mrs. Jefferies had the maids they had brought with them, those willing to stay in a household so far out, cleaning rooms before beds, bedding, and other necessary items were brought in and set up. There were quite a few bedrooms that weren't finished and that Mr. O'Grady would hear from him if they disturbed the family.

"Agatha, come with me," she said to the child and held out her hand.

The little girl happily skipped alongside her mother, but when the twins and Joseph would have tagged along, Abigail stopped them. "Oh no, you three stay with Brodie near the house," she told them, looking at her maid, who nodded and went to grab the two boys. Joseph was harder to grab as he knew he wasn't one of the lords, but he also knew better than to disobey in front her ladyship, pretending to obey in front of the woman. Two years older than the twins, he was mischievous and always the leader in their getting into things, usually a lot of trouble.

Before Abigail could head for the barns, Mrs. Fredericks stopped her. "What do you want us to do with 'er?" she asked, pointing at the Aboriginal woman, who still stared off into nothing.

Abigail, who had been so excited to arrive on the station, had forgotten the incident on the road in the small village. She glanced at the poor woman. "Well, please clean her up, find her some clothes, and put her to bed for now …" she left off as Mrs. Fredericks shook her head. "What?" she asked the housekeeper, surprised.

"We should have left her with her own kind," the woman stated in a disparaging voice.

"Her own kind?" she asked slowly. Agatha was tugging at her hand. "Just a minute Agatha," she ordered the young girl to halt her skipping and tugging on her arm.

"Thems should stay with their own," she stated, looking at the woman with a sneer.

"You realize she can hear you?" Agatha stopped her skipping at the tone in her mother's voice, staring between her mother and the governess who had helped raise her all these years and then to the Aboriginal woman who sat at the back of one of the wagons.

Mrs. Fredericks was shaking her head again. "I'm not so sure she can. Something is wrong with this one there is."

"This *one*?" Abigail asked, her tone becoming tighter.

Gesturing at the woman, she tried to plead her case. "There is something wrong here, and she don't speak no English," the woman stated. She made a gesture at her own head and circled her finger.

"Mrs. Fredericks, are you refusing to clean the woman up?" Abigail asked, astonished. She couldn't remember her acting this way before, but then she remembered Mrs. Fredericks' reaction to the Aboriginal people they met at Lawrence Station. Two of her Abigail's guards had been prejudiced as well. She recalled Leesa Fredericks avoiding her

eventual friend, Alinta, the wife of Mel. She hadn't been overt, but in this moment, she recalled all that, and it made her angry.

"I just think that those people should stay with their own. We don't need them here," the housekeeper stated, gesturing towards the wagon.

"I will have you know, one my best friends is an Aborigine woman, and I don't appreciate your attitude," she replied frostily. At this the woman showed her first sign that she understood them, glancing up and around covertly.

"It's all well and good for you, your ladyship, but people like me—" began Mrs. Fredericks, realizing her error.

"People like you?" she asked pointedly.

"Well, we don't have the luxury of keeping pets," she gestured at the woman disparagingly.

"Leesa Fredericks, in all the years I have known you, I have never seen such disrespect to guests in my home or people around me. I will have you pack up your things now, and you can return to Sydney with your son." She gestured at the boy, who was even now whispering things to her sons, probably inappropriate if she had to hazard a guess. Things she had found amusing in the past were now coming into sharp focus. Things she had forgiven as they were active young boys, she now realized that this boy, the instigator with her own sons, was actually causing them to behave in a manner which did not befit their station. As lords of the realm, some behavior could be overlooked, after all boys would be boys, but now she looked at the behavior, instigated by this boy, and realized it had to come to an end.

"You can't mean that, m'lady? After all these years of loyalty?" she gasped out, her hand going to her chest at the abruptness of all this.

Nodding and realizing a myriad of things she had overlooked from this servant, she did mean it. "I do," she admitted, glancing at one of the guards who nodded discretely. He would accompany the housekeeper and make certain she took nothing that wasn't her own. "The wagons will begin their return to the city, and if you wish to ride with them, you had better be ready or you will walk. You have received your wages for the year, and I will not ask for any of it back. Consider this your severance." She turned her back on the woman, dismissing the incident from her mind and turning to the Black woman. "Please, come with me, and we will see about getting you situated." She encouraged the woman to get out of the wagon and, once on the ground, steadied her. The woman looked astonished to have a White woman—especially *this* one—touch her.

Many of the servants who had been unloading the wagons had stopped when Mrs. Fredericks refused her ladyship and watched as the scene unfolded. One of them stepped forward. "I'll see to it, m'lady," Moll stated and glanced at the horrified Mrs. Fredericks. Taking her cue from her ladyship, she ignored her and glanced at the Black woman. "You can come with me," she offered in a kindly voice.

"Thank you, Moll," Abigail said, releasing the woman's arm and steering Agatha around the group and past the wagon. "Please take their lordships to the nursery," she ordered Brodie, nodding to her as she grabbed a hand of each of the now protesting young boys. They didn't yet realize their young friend was going to be leaving, and she didn't want a scene. She saw out of the corner of her eye as Mrs. Fredericks grabbed her own son's hand and yanked him towards the house, the guard following and three guards hurrying to catch up with

her ladyship. A fourth came out of the house soon after, jogging to catch up with them.

Agatha started skipping again, and Abigail breathed a sigh of relief as they headed across the lawns to the first barn. She didn't want the incident that had just unfolded to upset the little girl, but Abigail thought, with the resilience of youth, perhaps the little girl had already forgotten it. She was wrong, though. Children observed everything, and like sponges, they took it all in.

"Mama, is Mrs. Fredericks and Joseph leaving?" she asked as she skipped along.

Sighing at the occasion she would like to forget, she answered the little girl. "Yes, darling, they are."

"But why? Why wouldn't she help that poor woman get cleaned up?"

She realized the little girl had been aware of all the nuances of that distasteful scene. She wasn't going to sugarcoat it for her. "Because Mrs. Fredericks doesn't like Black people. She didn't want to help her."

The little girl thought about it for a while. "Tante Alinta is Aborigine, isn't she?"

"Yes, she is." She waited for the inevitable next question the girl would think up. She wasn't pleased to have this conversation because her anger was still there. She blamed it firmly on people like Mrs. Fredericks, but she knew that at one time she too might have been just as ignorant. It was up to her to teach her children that Blacks were people too and not lesser than.

"Aborigine people are Black, aren't they?"

"Yes, they are," she answered, wondering what she would ask next. It was kind of amusing and helped temper her anger at her former nursemaid turned housekeeper.

"Tante Alinta was nice; will this lady be nice?"

Surprised that she called the woman a lady, she smiled. "I don't know, but she's been badly abused and we must give her time to recover. Can you not pester her with questions until she can speak for herself?" She was certain her daughter was going to ask what abused meant, but when she didn't ask, Abigail was surprised.

"Of course, Mama," she promised and with that they were at the barn.

"M'lady, we is unpacking the wagons with the ducks, chickens, and geese," a man told her, thinking she was coming to see how far along they were, doffing his hat.

"I hope you're putting them in the pens first because if you release them right away, they won't know where they belong," she told him. She'd had her own servants keep the new livestock in the stables that no longer housed her Thoroughbreds until the day of their move to the station. She remembered how much fun she'd had taking her society ladies with her to the markets where the farmers brought their produce and livestock and buying some of the poultry she now saw being unloaded in the many cages. The women had never done such and had been fascinated by the market, their servants hovering behind them to buy up fruits and vegetables that the ladies wished. All were impressed by her ladyship's knowledge of the animals and birds she purchased for her station. They'd had so much fun that it was the talk of many gatherings, and those who hadn't gone lamented over the missed opportunity. So many had enjoyed the outing that several tried to

duplicate it, but without her ladyship's knowledge and presence, it wasn't as fun. Finally, they just sent their servants to do the buying.

"A few were put in the ponds, m'lady," he told her, looking alarmed.

"I suggest your men retrieve those fowl they can capture and put them in their pens, keeping them in the cages until the current occupants get used to them. There is a pecking order after all," she told him. As he nodded and hurried off, she shook her head. She'd had so much fun picking out and buying the chickens, ducks, and geese, she didn't want to lose any of them. She knew there would be natural decreases in their flocks, but she didn't want to lose them to sheer negligence. She spotted her stable manager. "Ah, Mr. Perry," she called, bringing the man to a halt from where he had been heading.

"Your ladyship," he said in return, doffing his hat respectfully.

"What's this I hear that her ladyship," she indicated Agatha, "cannot keep her pony in here?" She gestured about the large barn, the wooden stalls looking sharp with their shiny wood, a horse in almost every box stall.

"Well, I thought that we'd keep …" he began haltingly, realizing his error as soon as he saw the two of them. Of course, the child would tell on him.

"Her ladyship must be able to ride her pony," she continued as though he hadn't spoken. "The two lords as well when they are old enough for ponies. We have plenty of room in the many barns for my babies," she gestured to a few of the Thoroughbreds that grooms were washing and using brushes on. She knew each of their names, having ridden each and every one of them herself. She loved the freedom of raising these horses herself. Her father having dismissed her extensive

knowledge of horses and their bloodlines. She recalled briefly how impressed Mel's father had been and that he had actually listened to her, despite being a young girl.

"Of course, m'lady," he answered, realizing his place and resenting the interference of a child. "But don't you think—" he began in a reasonable voice that he used with trying women.

But she continued again as though he hadn't spoken. "Furthermore, the blacks from Twin Station I do want bred to my stallions," she indicated the barn that housed one of the stallions and the other barn further down the row, keeping the warm-blooded animals far away from each other so there wouldn't be problems. "I think we've discussed that before?" she warned him.

"Of course, m'lady," he acquiesced, annoyed that she wouldn't let him choose the breeding program. He had thought he would be in charge, but she knew the stud, she knew every horse, and she knew what she had sent for from England.

"How are the courses coming?" she asked next, letting go of Agatha's hand as she went to pet one of the horses that was tied in the aisle. She knew this horse would be gentle with the girl, and she watched as it leaned down as far as it ties would allow to sniff at the young girl, its tail flicking at flies and its shoulders shuddering in appreciation to the groom who was running a brush over it.

"We've got everything planted on the courses, and I must say there are some excellent fields," he enthused, relieved that she was no longer berating him. He was looking forward to sending horses down the various courses. "The oval is coming along as well, and we've gotten out all the rocks. I swear that field grows 'em."

"Well, let's make certain that crop of rocks is well gone. I won't have my horses going lame because we missed any. We'll have to plow it several times to make certain there are none near the surface. Especially after the rains."

"Of course, m'lady," he told her, resenting every bit of her instructions. As if he didn't know to have the grooms remove all the rocks from the track they were building for racing the Thoroughbreds, training them for the other track that she'd had built back in Parramatta, the only place that had room for such an endeavor. Already races had been held there several times, the horses from Brentford giving a good showing against others that competed. Others rented the track when Thoroughbred racing wasn't being offered. He was used to having full say in the stables he had managed back in England and having a woman—even a lady of the realm—instructing him, he disliked her interference.

Abigail wasn't stupid. She'd butted heads with this man from the day he arrived with more of her horses from England. Captain Scott had come to discuss business with her and to warn her that Mr. Perry was arrogant and full of opinions on her horses. Scott enjoyed bringing her animals to her, but also in his hold were foodstuffs, antiques, and passengers who helped pay for the crossing. Because of her ladyship, he had a life he loved and profits they could both share. She'd been more than fair in her dealings with him, and he'd be loyal to her, choosing men to captain her other ships that would prove to be just as loyal and just as profitable for their ventures. Seeing the behavior of the stable manager, he had warned her. Perry was certain he was in charge but finding that her ladyship was knowledgeable and informed

about those horses bred in England, and those she'd had transported to Australia, he was taken aback to realize he was to answer to her.

One of the things Scott had brought her was a copy of several of the books she had found in the library of the house in London. Worthington House had some fine books on Thoroughbreds, and she'd wanted to take them, but thought it better to leave them in the library there. Only now had she finally sent for copies, writing booksellers in London to find the books she wanted. Even now her servants were unpacking the boxes of books she had purchased, both from England and here in Australia to line the shelves of the library in her new home. She'd enjoyed finding books in the shops in Sydney, surprised when she found any on horses. There were many books she knew she would enjoy reading by the fire, waiting for the days when the weather was too inclement to go out and ride her babies.

Abigail let the man wander off to go about his duties as he saw fit. She knew that a woman knowing about horses irked some men, and he was one of them. She would have to try to get along with the man. He was good at his job, but his arrogance and assumptions just made it impossible. She watched as the horse nuzzled her daughter, one of the grooms having released its head so it could reach the little girl.

She stepped out of the barn, admiring the beauty of what O'Grady had built and then glancing at the rows of barns in various stages of completion. One of the barns in the middle row was completely empty so they could ride inside its cavernous depths out of the weather and work the various horses they were breeding on the station. It was twice as wide as the other barns, and the floor was covered in shavings, making it easier to clean up after the horses. She knew that Mr. Perry did not like the blacks from the Outback that Carmen had bred, but

Abigail was fascinated by these sturdy beasts, intending to breed some of their offspring with the fine Brumby's she had acquired. The first breeding, though, would be to her carefully chosen Thoroughbred stallions, much to Mr. Perry's annoyance. She had promised these offspring to not only Carmen but Mel because they were all fascinated with fine horseflesh and the results of each of their breeding programs. Some of these very horses had been owned first by Victor Lawrence and then, when he passed away, by Mel before they had been sold off to Lord Worthington, Abigail's husband. She'd had to plant the idea in his head because he too would not listen to a mere woman about horses. After all, what could a young woman such as Abigail know about horses? She and Carmen and Mel could talk about horses until they bored Fabiola and Alinta to death. It amused Abigail to remember the many conversations with her old friend. She missed those women and decided to write to them both tonight, telling of the move to the station.

She shook her head, amazed at how beautiful the home paddock was. She looked back at the house, the very large house that she'd had built with its many secrets. Even now a wagonload of wood was driving up to it to be unloaded into the unfinished parts of the house. She knew the wood had been cut in the village she had established, taking over what had been a sleepy little hamlet along the creek that led from her own ponds, where the second of her two wood mills had been put in. The villagers had appreciated the work because their own small farms could use the wood and they benefited from the jobs made available to their offspring. The men had dug a small pond with a dam to trap the creek and power the wheel that turned the blades in the mill. A second mill had sprung up across from it, using its own wheel to

power the large stones that crushed the grains that farmers from all over the area came to depend on. Having a gristmill in the little village had caused quite a sensation, and Abigail had been pleased when the villagers asked to name the village Brentford after her station and son. She had, instead, so there was no confusion, suggested calling it Brentwood, for the many trees that were growing along the pond, many that were planted by her own men on the land she had acquired for the two different mills. The villagers were grateful for the businesses she had provided and the ones that would follow, so they acquiesced to her suggestion,

So much had been done in so few years, and she was pleased with their progress. They weren't done—not by a long shot—and she knew she had many ideas she wanted to see come to fruition. But right now she was pleased with the progress she could see, especially here on the station. Already their first foals were being born in their own box stalls and would later run with the mares in their own paddocks. She looked at the gardens along the lawns that led down to the barns, far enough from the house that they wouldn't smell the animals that she loved. She saw one of the farmers she had hired walking a cow down the lane in back of one of the barns, heading for fields designated for dairy cows. She heard the bleating of a sheep but couldn't see them as they were on the hills beyond the barns, hidden by the foliage of the many trees she had insisted they keep. She also heard the many birds she loved to watch, the brilliant colors in their plumage confusing her as she attempted to learn the various species.

"Mama, can we go and look?" Agatha gestured to where hammering was coming from one of the barns down the lane.

"Of course, my darling," she agreed, her anger and annoyances forgotten as she took her daughter's hand and walked with her. The atmosphere of this place put her at peace. She felt, finally, that she was home.

CHAPTER FIFTEEN

Mrs. Fredericks' firing shocked the whole household. By the time the young Lady Worthington and the Countess of Worthington returned from their sojourn down to the barns, the wagons had been unloaded and Mrs. Fredericks and her son Joseph and their few possessions were gone. The lords, both Worthington and Brentford, were upset over losing their friend. They'd known Joseph all their lives and didn't know what to do with themselves but act up over his leaving. With servants still putting things away from the wagons, the house was in an uproar. Whispered conversations halted suddenly as Abigail walked through the house, to make certain things were put in their proper places. If she could summarily fire Mrs. Fredericks, a long-time and trusted servant, who else could go?

"Where is the woman we brought with us from the village?" she asked a servant in passing.

"M'lady?" he answered, visibly nervous at being addressed directly.

"The woman who was brought in the wagons with us?"

"I don't know, m'lady," he admitted, feeling he had failed her.

"Well, don't you think you should find out for me?" she asked, annoyed. What was wrong with everyone? She couldn't miss the immediate silence that kept assaulting her as she walked through the rooms of the large house. Servants suddenly becoming quiet and then quite busy as she passed. It was starting to wear on her nerves, and she was developing a headache. She watched as the man ran off to find out for her.

"M'lady," Mr. Jefferies approached her, bowing slightly.

"Yes, Mr. Jefferies, everything in the house now?"

"Yes, M'lady, it is. Are you inspecting that it all has been put away correctly?" he asked knowingly.

"Yes, and we will need a few pieces as they finish." She pointed to where they couldn't help but hear hammers and she had seen the cut wood being brought in a side door and rushed up the servants staircase.

"If they are making too much noise, I can …"

"No, no, we knew there would be finishing touches," she understated. There were whole rooms that weren't finished, but the men were working like ants, crawling over every inch of those areas to finish her home. She was just pleased that enough was finished so they could live there. They could put up with the minor inconveniences of finishing off the other rooms.

"M'lady, in lieu of today's incident …" he began, careful of his wording.

Annoyed at having it brought up again when she'd managed to put it from her, she immediately felt her pique begin again. It showed on her face as she turned to her butler, her eyebrow raised.

Seeing she was not happy with him, he quickly added, "You will be in need of a housekeeper. May I put forth my missus for the position?"

Knowing that frequently happened—she herself had seen where a housekeeper, the highest in the hierarchy of servants on the women's side, and the butler, the highest in the household servants on the men's side, married—she wasn't surprised at the request. The only reason she hadn't given Mrs. Jefferies the position when she hired the butler was because she had promised it to Mrs. Fredericks, who had been in her household since she hired on as wet-nurse to the twins. However, she wasn't fond of Mrs. Jefferies and already regretted that she'd had to dismiss Mrs. Fredericks. The woman had been loyal to her sons, and she'd anticipated the woman would someday run her son's household. Disappointed in how things had turned out, she wasn't ready to replace the woman.

"I'll think about it," she demurred, immediately exasperating the butler, who had thought it the logical conclusion to the situation. After all, his wife was a trained housekeeper and keeping her as an upper maid had been a step down for her. Still, the Brentford household wasn't that large, and now that they were out at the station, they would have to hire more servants. It was a foregone conclusion, at least to him, that his wife would be elevated to her rightful position. She was already training new maids as this house was much larger. He too was training footmen for the big house.

"Of course, m'lady," he said, bowing. "Dinner will be served shortly."

"Thank you," she said, making her way up the sweeping stairs to her rooms. She loved what O'Grady had done here, making two master suites with a large sitting room between them. In the sitting room was a set of bookcases that held her personal reading materials and swung open to reveal a hidden staircase. It led both downstairs and up to the third floor, where the guest rooms were, and then up to the attics where the servants' quarters were. These were finished off, several of the servants having their own private rooms depending on the hierarchy in the house. Some would share since there was no reason for a lowly maid to have a private room. Half of the servants' quarters were for men, half for the women. In the middle were married couples' quarters, such as those for Mr. and Mrs. Jefferies. Since the house was new, there was room for more servants and couples' quarters. Mr. and Mrs. Jefferies also served as chaperones, so there was no fraternizing between the quarters. Already the hastily vacated quarters of Mrs. Fredericks were being speculated on, but since there wasn't a replacement, the room was hastily cleaned and closed.

Abigail had made her way down this secret staircase many times, down to the basement to obtain a bottle of a fine Australian wine from her growing collection. She'd been introduced to such wines by the MacArthurs from their estate called Camden Park. She had also had Scott import wines from England, France, and even South Africa. Her cellars were becoming quite extensive as she tried new vintages. She even hoped to find someone to grow her own vintage on Brentford. She'd sent out feelers through Captain Scott, dropping a word here and there with the vintners he dealt with around the world.

As she dressed for dinner, she wondered how one went about finding a person who could cultivate the grapes that would be needed to

start their own press. It would take many years to have a wine worthy of Brentford, but that was why she was impatient. Already, she had been in Australia for years, and finding these people would take time. She'd had her gardeners cultivate the juniper berries that Carmen had imparted to her, expressing a desire for the berries that would result from those plants. She couldn't grow them in the heat of the Outback, but perhaps, here in the Blue Mountains, with its cold winters, they might grow. Already several plants were growing from the berries she'd carefully meted out to them, holding some back in case they killed them. Carmen had confessed that juniper berries were necessary for the fine gin that the woman produced. Brentford already had several bottles of the rare treat in its stores. She'd had them make a garden, high on the mountain, enclosed so that no stray animals might eat the plants that were carefully planted against a future crop for Carmen.

O'Grady was building her a beautiful arboretum. It captured the warm rays of the sun from the north. When she'd objected at its design, pointing out that the south facing sun was hotter, he reminded her she was in Australia now and that things were upside down here. The north facing sun was hotter below the equator. She'd laughed at her folly, glad that her builder knew so much more than she. Fortunately, the sun still rose in the east and set in the west, so she wasn't too upset at being wrong.

Dinner was not formal here in the house, but she did dress nicely, pleased that Brodie was able to get Agatha, Auggie, and Mel dressed for dinner so they could continue learning their manners that were so important. The boys chattered on about various things, and when she was able to get a word in edgewise, Agatha contributed, mostly about

the barns and horses they had seen that day. Both boys clamored to go down to the barns after hearing this. "Settle down, settle down," their mother cautioned, pleased to be eating this fine meal with her little family.

She wondered when the house and gardens would be far enough along that she could hold her promised weekend party. She'd inspect the unfinished parts of the house tomorrow to ascertain her plans. She was pleased when the children didn't bring up Mrs. Fredericks or Joseph at the dinner table. Taking a walk after dinner, they listened to the animals surrounding them and enjoyed the sun as it set over their beautiful land and slid down behind the Blue Mountains. Although it had been early for dinner, she didn't like eating late and going to bed on a full stomach; this walk helped to aid in digestion and to tire the children out. She had to pull the boys back from racing down to the barns because they were eager to have the same adventures Agatha had had earlier.

She watched as Brodie shepherded the three of them off to wash up before bed, mentally remembering to ask Mr. Jefferies to assign a maid to assist her in the future, now that Mrs. Fredericks was no longer with them. She sighed. It would be a long time before she could forget the incident of today.

"M'lady, Kaleena is asking to see you?" one of the servants asked.

"Who?" she asked in return, unfamiliar with the name.

"Kaleena, the woman you helped earlier today?"

It was then that she realized the servant was being diplomatic, and the reason the name was unfamiliar was because she hadn't heard it before. It must be the name of the Aboriginal woman. "Yes, where is she?"

"We put her in the servants' quarters, unless you want her moved?"

"No, that's okay," she answered, heading for the main stairs and following as the servant hurried up before her. "How is she faring?" she asked as they climbed.

"She was right tuckered out after she was bathed, but some of the maids lent her some clothing, and after a good nap, she was quite famished. Mrs. Harris saw her fed, and Brodie made certain she was comfortable."

Abigail filed that in her head, making certain she would thank both women for their compassion, something that had been sadly absent in Mrs. Fredericks. She hadn't really noticed before, but now that she thought about it, Mrs. Fredericks had lacked compassion for anyone she thought beneath her.. Joseph too had a quality about him that Abigail had ignored, but now she was relieved her sons wouldn't be exposed to his unruly influence. They could come up with their own naughtiness instead of being egged on by the older boy.

"Are the servants' quarters adequate? Everyone settled?" she asked as they walked up another flight of stairs, well away from the main staircase and off to a side of the house, out of the way and sight of the main household and behind an inconspicuous door. This led to the staircase to the attics where the servant's quarters were. The stairway split off to the left and right, depending on whether the servant were male or female and the couples quarters could be accessed from either and she was pleased to see the closed doors on the used rooms, especially those where the only married couple, her butler and his wife lived. She looked into the unused rooms along the women's side as they walked.

"Oh yes, m'lady, they are right nice. Warm and dry. It's all so new and clean," she gushed, wanting to ensure her ladyship knew how grateful they all were for the nice accommodations. The entire attic floor was taken up by servants quarters, which were fairly large and spacious compared to other households that many had worked in. O'Grady hadn't put in the luxuries that were on the first, second, and third floors, but they did have two bathing rooms with a toilet, one for the men and one for the women. It was unheard of to have indoor facilities such as these, and they were all in awe of using such. The couples quarters had their own bathing room along with a toilet to share when there would be other couples working in this establishment. Even down at the barracks, they had modern plumbing they could share, and all were grateful that her ladyship had instructed the builder to put such amenities in. Having to trudge out to a separate bathing house or use a dunny with the possibility of snakes and spiders that could bite and kill you had alarmed those who were from England.

"Good, I hope everyone is settling in," she responded, feeling winded from all the steps. She stopped outside the room the maid indicated. The door was wide open, and a woman lay propped up on the cot within. "Hello. Are you okay?" she asked the woman.

"Ah yes, I right now," the woman pidgined, English obviously not her first language. But then a lot of Whites tended to speak in halting English to Aboriginal people, encouraging them to speak like this. "I want to thank ye for your help today," she stated, attempting to get up, although Abigail could see it pained her.

"No, no, you stay there," she stated immediately and quickly sat down on the edge of the cot. "You have enough to eat?" she asked, seeing her tray was still quite full.

"Yes, plenty eat. I ask that I work here, perhaps?"

"You would like to work here?" she asked, automatically correcting the woman's English as she had heard Mel do to Alinta many times over the months she had stayed there.

The woman nodded. "I right clean for you?"

"You would like to clean my house for me?" she asked, again correcting her. At the woman's nod, she asked, "Do you have other skills?"

The woman frowned, not sure what she meant.

"Do you do anything other than clean?" Abigail could almost read the woman's mind as she thought about what she had done for the man who claimed to be her husband.

"I's cooks too."

Abigail judged her English to be different than Alinta's. Perhaps the way people spoke around her made her learn it a different way. Alinta never resented Mel's correcting her, but then she was always willing to improve herself for Mel. She wanted to please her mate. This woman had been abused and degraded by that man; maybe she didn't want to learn.

"Well, for now you just rest and heal. We will see later what you might do for us," she answered diplomatically, not certain the woman would stay. She would have to see what the magistrate would do about this situation. Beating an Aboriginal woman wouldn't mean much to some, but Abigail refused to allow it in her presence or on her station. She certainly didn't want the woman abused and would defend her, keeping her safe here in her own home. She bestowed a smile on the woman, and after a moment the woman returned it with a hint of her own, her teeth very white against her dark skin. "They tell me your

name is Kaleena?" At the woman's hesitant nod, she asked, "Did I pronounce that correctly?" She knew she had probably butchered it, but at the woman's hesitancy, she wanted to clarify.

Kaleena corrected her, pronouncing it with the full inflection of her tribe. "Kaa-leen-aa," she told her, rolling the l and stressing the ee's. "But yous cans call me Martha."

"Is that the name that man gave you?" she asked and saw as the woman lost her smile and became sad again. At the woman's nod Abigail added, "No, we will call you Kaleena and learn to pronounce it correctly," she added with a laugh. The woman looked up at her, surprised. "I'll let you rest; you just take your time," Abigail stated and leaned forward to pat the woman's hand. The Aboriginal woman pulled her own hand back out of reflex, unused to someone touching her who wasn't going to hurt her. Abigail looked shocked and then softened as she realized the reason for the woman's withdrawal. "You just rest and heal," she told the woman slowly, showing none of the anger welling inside her that someone, anyone, *that man* could inflict such suffering on the woman. She smiled again, got up, and left the room.

As Abigail left, a servant hurried in. "Are you done with this, or would you like me to leave it?" She indicated the tray with half the food still on it.

Afraid she wouldn't get more food she said, "Leave it." The servant nodded and left the room, closing the door gently. Kaleena waited to see if she would lock it but heard none of the tell-tale sounds of a locked door. She stared at the door for a long time, thinking about the encounter with that strange White woman who had defended her earlier today and then this one, who had brought her home, had her bathed and

clothed, and allowed her to be fed and given a bed. She looked about the small room with its three empty beds and wondered at this strange world.

"Make certain that the others treat her nicely," Abigail warned the servant as they headed down the stairs. "I will brook no one treating her badly."

"Of course, m'lady," she stated. After Mrs. Fredericks' dismissal, no one would dare, even if they felt resentment for the Black woman's presence or felt she shouldn't be in the main house, that blacks should be segregated to their own spaces. The servant herself hoped the woman would stay and was good at cleaning. They needed more servants in a house this large, even if most of it was unused.

Abigail was tired and hurried off to the nursery, where Agatha, Auggie, and Mel had adjoining rooms with beds set up. They were all in the room together, Brodie sitting wearily in a chair. "I'll just pop out for a moment," she whispered as Abigail came in to read. The children were soundly asleep, the result of a very full day, and Abigail was feeling it herself. She checked that each was tucked in correctly, smiling at Auggie, who was lying on his back, spread out, with his mouth wide open, whereas Mel was cuddled in, his hand near his mouth, probably to suck his thumb. She'd have to remember to have the servants start sprinkling pepper on it to get him to stop; they didn't want him to have misshapen teeth, and he was old enough to stop that habit. Agatha lay soundly asleep in the middle of her bed, almost as though she had lain back and gone right to sleep.

She smiled fondly at each of the children, feeling richer than Midas at the moment and happier than she could remember since … since … she had loved Mel that one year. They'd been so happy until they'd

been discovered by her father. That part had been horrible, and she'd shoved those memories down into a hole and attempted to forget. But she couldn't. It was part of her past and who she'd become. Marrying her off to Lord Worthington had given her these three beautiful children. He had been so much older than she, his death had been a good thing. They were hers, completely and totally.

CHAPTER SIXTEEN

Getting the house sorted, furniture tried out and moved and then moved again, took days. There was more they needed. She had been careful not to overbuy, so there was still a lot to purchase and she enjoyed buying things. The servants developed a good attitude, even humor, as she laughed over where to put this desk, this table, or that lamp, where to hang the paintings she had acquired, and how to organize the entire household. There were still the sounds of building as O'Grady and his men hurried to finish the large house. Abigail often escaped the noise to walk in her growing gardens or to head down to the stables to ride.

"Mama, can I go with you?" Agatha pleaded on more than one occasion.

"Is your schoolwork done for the day?" she would ask. She wouldn't allow the girl to miss out on her education. Finding a tutor willing to teach her ladyship—and then later the twins—had proved difficult, but the one she had found was eager and willing to teach a girl. Abigail had made certain he wasn't stinting the knowledge he was imparting because she knew some men didn't think a girl could learn like a boy. She was pleased with the young girl's progress thus far and looked forward to the boys starting. In fact, the tutor had allowed them to sit in on occasion, letting them soak up the knowledge he imparted in the form of stories like the little sponges they were.

When Agatha wasn't busy with her studies, Abigail and she rode about the station, inspecting the various farmers' fields, seeing the animals and their offspring, laughing at the wallabies and kangaroos that hopped about. Abigail cautioned the child more than once to avoid the kangaroos, especially the big louts who were as large as a man and equally muscled. Occasionally, the grooms had to shoot a particularly belligerent buck if he became too aggressive and couldn't be frightened off. Roast kangaroo was not a bad meal, as Abigail had learned out at Lawrence Station. She gave standing orders to kill all dingoes and feral hogs; she didn't want to have to worry about such things for herself, her children, or her valuable horses, much less her people. She would have thought that here in civilization, with so many people about, the animals would be frightened away, but they were adaptable and sneaky. She often forgot in the little kingdom she was establishing how remote they still were. She told her farmers and the grazers to shoot them on sight; she couldn't afford to let them become established on the station.

Checking on the fencing program that was still going on about the large chunk of land she had purchased, she saw where roads were going

in, some of them across otherwise dry creeks and ditches. "We'll have to put in drains so the road doesn't wash away," she mentioned to her guards so they could point it out to her groundskeeper. Not just the gardeners worked on such things, and she had many men who worked on the station doing these types of tasks.

In the months after moving to the station, she was pleased to receive correspondence from her friends in the Outback and those in Sydney. Captain Scott grouched that he had to travel two days just to see her now, but he admired the fine home she now lived in. It definitely was in accordance to her station in life. Their shipping business had some setbacks, losing one of their ships to a storm off the Cape as it rounded Africa. Those were treacherous waters in the best of times, but he suspected the captain, who had gone down with his ship and all his passengers, and a couple of horses of her ladyships, hadn't realized how treacherous the waters could be. His own ship had brought a couple more horses, this time warm-blooded Holsteins from Germany along with a breed he couldn't pronounce that were called Cold Bloods. He knew her ladyship was hoping to breed Hanoverians, which were a result of these cold-blooded horses, with Thoroughbreds. Two of his ships had brought pure-blooded Merinos that were even now in the hills above the station, grazing down the tall grasses that grew there. There had been some envious grazers who had attempted to purchase the Merinos when Scott's men temporarily put them in pens in Sydney, and he had been hard put to get them down Parramatta Road with the hired jackaroos.

"It is a fair ride," she admitted, having built a house in Parramatta for that very reason. If she had to travel to Sydney on business, she could rest there, especially in inclement weather. The train between

Parramatta and Sydney was nearly built, and when it was finished, she might not need the house but was holding on to it. In fact, she was having several like it built to take advantage of the anticipated housing market. Some of the men were no longer necessary on the station, so O'Grady had sent them to start these projects, including the second mill that was well on its way to being complete. A fire had damaged a couple of the houses for workers at the mill, but the kitchen that had started the fire was the only thing lost and her builders had quickly repaired these houses. She was considering a townhouse in Sydney for when they needed to travel all that way but hadn't seen anything she liked. She knew that O'Grady would build one for her if she asked him and acquired the land. She'd have to think on that project since he had so much yet to build.

Captain Scott had found her in her coach house, looking at the new coach she had ordered all the way from England. It was similar to the Worthington coach that had come so far from the estate it originally belonged to. She'd sent it back, instructing the men to put it away until her son was of age to use it. This new coach had a different coat of arms, the Brentford design having been put up all over the estate, including the barns where a large coat of arms representing the family hung on each front of the barns. The smaller placards on the house had been replaced so everything here on the estate was to reflect Brentford and not Worthington. It had been subtle and she hadn't made a big deal of it, but the children had noticed and asked about it. She had gently explained that this was Brentford and that Worthington was in England. She had also explained, and didn't think the boys understood yet, that Auggie was the Earl of Worthington and that Mel was the Earl of Brentford. She wanted to instill pride in both of them, but she also

didn't want Auggie or Agatha to feel unwelcome here. This was their home, but she told stories about Worthington so that they didn't feel left out.

"This is mighty impressive," the captain stated, looking at her coach and two carriages. He knew she rode horseback whenever she could, the carriages too slow and the lumbering coach almost a glacial pace to her. Still, she must keep up appearances, and there were times when the coach and carriages were necessary, especially with the children so young. But he actually meant the building itself, its rich and beautiful woods gleaming in the sunlight. The building could accommodate more than she had here. There were a couple of wagons inside as well, but they were for the home paddock use and she could always borrow from her farmers on the estate if she needed another.

"It is beautiful," she stated but she wasn't looking at her new coach now either. "O'Grady did himself proud," she told him, enjoying each of the barns as she realized they all had their own unique flavor and personality. Despite looking nearly identical from the outside, once you entered one of them, it felt different. Whether it was for the horses or for the equipment they needed to maintain this large estate, each building were built to last. That would be put to the test this year as they entered a particularly nasty rainy season with high winds and torrential rains that would flatten poorly built buildings and homes.

"That man's buildings are definitely becoming well-known," he acceded, wishing that O'Grady could build in Sydney too, they needed a decent office down by the wharf they owned, perhaps building a new wharf too, but he was still too busy finishing things up for the countess. He'd heard a few people wishing they could entice the Irishman away, but the man was loyal to her ladyship. In all the years it had taken to

build this complex series of barns, the main house, and those in Parramatta with the mills, the man had found quality workers, those he could promote and trust to do the work in the manner in which he saw fit. He knew what the countess wanted, demanded really, and would accommodate her to the best of his and others' abilities.

Captain Scott spent a delightful weekend with the countess talking over business, making plans, and discussing whatever she wished to discuss. It was how he knew she wanted certain flowers that he could watch for when he was back in England and purchase large quantities to fill her gardens and gift to her friends. Already she had quite a rose garden as he admired it when they took walks in it, but some plants couldn't handle the heat of Australia and others were running wild even though the gardeners attempted to keep them in check. Her arboretum was filling with plants that couldn't handle the hot Australian sun. The captain enjoyed visiting with the woman. Her children were precocious, and he could see the men that the boys would become. He anticipated being the one to man the ship that would eventually take the boys, and possibly the young lady, back to England someday to attend school or go back to Hedgerows, the estate that Lord Worthington owned. He hadn't seen it, but he'd heard the stories her ladyship told the children, instilling in them the family pride. He knew what her ladyship was doing and he approved. She was still a young woman, and he often wondered if she would remarry, but she seemed so devoted to her children.

Through the expensive and hard to obtain windows of her arboretum, Abigail watched the new gardener she had hired to keep the plants lush without overwhelming the space. He sought her ladyship out to talk enthusiastically to her about the citrus he was growing for their table. "That there Kaleena knows a lot about native plants and has shown me what ones I can bring indoors and what is to stay outside," he told her, showing her the various plants as he explained.

With a bit of surprise, Abigail thought about the maid who had escaped the clutches of that man who called himself her husband and turned out to have enslaved her instead. She'd been cleaning the house in the many months she lived here, quite cheerfully, grateful for her position. One of the other maids who objected to her presence in the house had asked why Kaleena couldn't live in the barracks or down in an Aboriginal village, but Abigail had made it clear she would tolerate no prejudice or abuse against any Aboriginals. After all, they had lived here first. This had been further backed up by an incident when she was out riding. Three Aboriginal men were walking across a meadow on one of the higher elevations where she and her guards were riding, choosing to work one of her Hanoverians as she got used to the different breeds she had imported and intend to cross.

"I'll get rid of 'em," one of the guards promised her upon seeing the men.

"Wait, what?" she asked, surprised at his statement.

"Yeah, we been running them off. They should know better," another of the guards stated.

Abigail exchanged a look with her captain who happened to be part of her four-guard party that day. When the Aboriginal men saw them, they began to run and the two guards went to give chase. Abigail gave

heels to her mount, shocking it as she had never shown anything but kindness to it before. It sprang ahead.

"Wait! Stop!" she called to her guards but was ignored. She got near her one guard, lifting her foot below his stirrup and pushing him at the same time, unseating him from his mount. She saw as her captain grabbed the reins of the other guard who would have run these people off. The Aborigine's men stopped at the tree line to watch.

"How dare you?" she raged at the man she had unseated as he slowly got up from the ground. He was equally angry over being treated in such a manner, but his anger turned to puzzlement at the countess's cross words. "These people were here before us, and they deserve your respect! How *dare* you?" she bellowed, her anger causing her voice to raise. She turned to the other man. "And you, you should know better as well," she raged at the second man, shaking a finger at him. "Take care of this," she ordered her captain and then turned towards the trees, walking her horse slowly now, keeping it well in hand with her strong hands on the reins. The fourth guard shadowed her warily. He agreed with the other two guards but wasn't stupid enough to say so aloud, especially in her ladyship's presence. She had made it clear that Blacks were welcome on their estate, and while there weren't many working there—one maid and a couple of grooms—she would not allow them to be abused in any way. They kept mostly to themselves, but he knew that some of the Whites resented them being treated equally.

"Are you okay?" she asked the three men. She looked at the path they had been traveling, wondering if it were a song trail because Alinta had explained that her people, all Aboriginal people, had them.

These were ancient trails that crisscrossed the continent, and that the people used to travel from place to place.

They looked at her warily, and she wondered if any of them understood English. Then one older than the other two spoke haltingly. "We … be … fine, missus."

"I am so sorry. I didn't know my men were chasing your people off," she said earnestly, hoping they understood. She could see them exchange looks of surprise and hoped they understood her words. "Please, accept my apologies for my men. Your people are welcome here."

"These our lands," he stated, gesturing to the meadow.

She nodded, biting her lip and wondering how to explain. "I suppose they were, but I have purchased them from the government here in Australia." She couldn't explain about the bank. "I'm sure they took them from your people, but I would offer compensation. What can I do?"

His face showed no expression as he looked to his companions. He looked back to the White woman and shrugged. "What … can … you … do?" he asked.

"Surely I could do something?" she asked sincerely, feeling awful. "Perhaps I could purchase the lands from your people?"

He got a crafty look on his face at that question and held out his hand.

Realizing her mistake she shook her head. "No, I would have to speak with your … elders," she added ingeniously. "So that all your people would understand that these are my lands now."

"We no come here no more?" one of the others spoke up, and the first one put down his hand.

"No, I didn't say that. I don't mind you walking on the lands," she gestured to the trail and asked, "on your song trails?"

He looked surprised that she knew what it was.

She could see his expression, despite their attempts to remain impassive. "My friend Alinta told me of your ancient song trails. I respect them and want you to continue using them. Just don't remove my fences; climb over them where they cross?"

He studied her for a while, surprised to hear the name that sounded like a name an Aborigine would have. But no name knew, his language was different. Perhaps she was lying to them and had heard the name at one time. He nodded slightly, gesturing with his hand at the same time.

She smiled at the gesture and remembered how Mel had explained that it meant he agreed, that she hadn't realized Alinta was even making that gesture when they spoke. It had taken a long time to get her to nod or shake her head so that White people would understand her. Obviously, this man had been in contact with Whites before, not only to speak English but to know that both gestures were necessary.

"I don't want problems with your people. They are welcome to use the trails as they always have." She glanced at the first man, the one so ready to take money and then back to the others standing there. "I would welcome your elders to speak of my using and keeping these lands." She gestured amongst the meadows and beyond. Her horse shifted, and they looked at her warily. "I want no problems with your people," she repeated. "I will tell my people," she motioned to her men, the two who would have chased them off, both back behind her quite a way, the one back on his horse. "To no longer chase your people when using the trails," she gestured to where it was faintly

visible through the grasses. "If your people have problems with mine," she indicated herself and her men, "please come see me and I will try to help. I am the Countess of Worthington, Lady Worthington," she introduced herself. She could see it was probably too much, but she was sincere and hoped they would understand.

The men studied her for a long time. From the stockman's hat she was wearing to the Outback shirt and britches she favored when riding about her lands to her face, where she hoped they could tell she was being earnest. Finally, the second one gestured again and nodded at the same time. They all gave her one more intense look before turning and disappearing into the brush as her captain of the guard drew near.

Abigail turned to her men and observed that three of them had looks of revulsion and anger on their faces. Her captain looked concerned.

"Captain, you will handle this?" she asked, becoming brisk.

He nodded, and glanced at his men, who immediately schooled their faces. They were certain they were about to be admonished for their behavior.

"All three," she murmured as she rode past and he turned to get in line beside her.

"All?" he murmured back and saw her nod as they joined the three guards. He sighed inwardly but knew she wouldn't tolerate such behavior towards Blacks. It wasn't the first time she had fired someone for this behavior, and it probably wouldn't be the last. He'd seen how friendly she had become with that grazer's wife in the Outback. Lawrence Station had been a kingdom unto itself and quite different than anything he and his men had experienced in their lives. Although she wasn't trying to reproduce that here, he could see how the wife of the grazer becoming her friend had influenced her. He knew he would

be looking for three new guards by the end of the day. He wouldn't warn the other men, but he would let them know why those men had been let go. He'd let them make their own decisions from that.

Abigail considered the incident with the three men as she thought about Kaleena and what she would do with her. She hadn't needed much training to become a good maid for the household, but here too she'd had to let go of some of her people because they wouldn't work companionably with the Black woman. She'd replaced them, which was difficult since they lived out so far, but good wages and working for the countess was a matter of prestige among the hierarchy of servants. Getting dismissed from such a position made it quite difficult to find another job. She wondered if Kaleena would make a better gardener than a maid and determined to discuss it with her at the first opportunity. She knew Kaleena would do her best wherever Abigail put her, but Abigail wanted her to be well-suited and happy in her position.

CHAPTER SEVENTEEN

The invitations were highly sought after. The Countess of Worthington was holding a weeklong party at her new estate, Brentford, out past Parramatta near the Blue Mountains. Abigail had them printed on expensive paper stock with raised lettering. The full colors of the Worthington crest with the Brentford crest beside it made it look quite prestigious and impressive. Abigail had those two crests embossed not only on the invitations, but on a large placard that was framed in the hallway to show their roots were Worthington, but this home was Brentford.

For the first time, all the bedrooms in Brentford were to be used, and she had been hard put to furnish all of them completely, necessitating trips to Sydney and importing several important pieces of furniture. Those whose invitations hadn't included rooms on the estate

were taking up every available room in tiny villages from Brentwood to far off Parramatta. Those not realizing that the larger town of Parramatta was still some thirty miles away hastened to correct their mistakes by camping out closer to Brentford so they wouldn't miss the much-heralded party.

The governor and his wife were among the first to arrive.

"My lord … your ladyship," Maisy said as she curtsied to the countess, her daughter, and her sons. "This is so grand." She was in awe of the house, which was like nothing she had seen in Sydney. She'd been in the finest houses, including the governor's mansion, and still this house was more impressive somehow. It wasn't bigger, but something about it, with its turrets and cupolas, spoke of grandeur and wealth. Her ladyship hadn't been bragging as she told of the build. She gazed at the many chandeliers, especially the huge one found just inside the seven-foot-door-entranceway. Abigail had imported it all the way from Ireland. All the chandeliers sparkled in the bright Australian Outback sunshine. "It's breathtaking," she understated.

Abigail smiled. She'd been waiting for this party for many years and finally felt the estate, the house, and where she was at was such that she could invite all these people to show it off. "I owe my architect and my builder so much for helping me create my vision."

"Is this like Hedgerows?" the governor asked, wondering if he had misheard about the estate that the Worthington family owned in England.

"Oh, not at all," she denied, trying not to show her irritation. "Hedgerows is so much older and grand in its own right. Since this will be my younger son's estate, I wanted it different and more … unique," she finished mysteriously, hoping not to give anything away.

She wasn't about to explain to these people, to anyone, that Hedgerows had been dismal and a prison to her in her younger years, that she wanted nothing to do with it ever again. Since Auggie would someday inherit it all, she would never disparage it and, in fact, told all the children delightful stories about the place, even if she had to make some of it up.

"Well, I think you have succeeded," he told her ingeniously. He had bent over her hand, kissed the back, and smiled at her ladyship. This house was a testament to her fortitude. He thought her asking for land, for men, and constant favors would never end. However, he had been repaid for the many favors he bestowed on her with letters of thanks and many favors in return. He'd been surprised at the people she knew back in England who had written to him. He didn't know she'd had Sir Boardman contact the right people in London who could help this governor and his career, putting a word in the right circles. She'd further done the same with Mr. Cherwin at her mills, having him talk with certain other managers and business owners about what the governor had *helped* her achieve here in Australia for the colony and its people. They'd been careful about who was told; after all, she didn't want word leaking back to her father or brother. But she supposed someday that would be inevitable.

As Abigail spoke with the MacArthurs, pleased that John and Elizabeth had made the trip, she was so delighted to hear John state that he needed to speak with her gardeners to learn where they had gotten some of the plants he saw in her gardens and arboretum. Since his own gardens and estate had inspired her, she was quite honored that he thought there was something he could learn from hers.

So many people came that it helped alleviate the sadness she felt from no one from Twin Station or Lawrence Station attending. It was simply too far for a mere party, and both had sent letters thanking her for the invitations but declining and begging her to understand. She did, but she was disappointed, having wanted to show off her years of hard work. She'd admired both their stations, which were massive kingdoms, and she'd wanted them to see her own estate, now that it was coming along to her satisfaction. She'd written in response to their regrets that they were welcome anytime and that, should they find the need to come to Sydney, to stop or stay at Brentford.

While she wouldn't be holding a formal hunt for her week of activities, those that did know how to ride and had brought their mounts, a few she lent a couple of her precious Thoroughbreds to so they could all try out the courses that they had laid out on the estate. Riding along, jumping the obstacles, the hedges, the water hazards, and logs, she hoped her people and she had created courses that the guests would enjoy. She too laughed when she was unseated and wound up in the water, covered in mud. Her riding skirts were streaming as she climbed out laughing. She was relieved she wasn't hurt; the water had cushioned what could have been a bad fall. She wasn't the only one, and Many of the other riders found the courses tricky, but they followed her lead and faced the hazards with a sense of humor.

For those who were inclined to bet, she had staged races between her Thoroughbreds, sometimes against each other, sometimes against the other breeds she was attempting to propagate. There really was no contest between the other breeds and her pampered Thoroughbreds, but it was amusing to watch. Those who had acquired horses from her or imported their own even offered to race against her jockeys. It was an

interesting week, and she ended up purchasing two more Thoroughbreds she'd not known were in Australia but knew of their pedigrees from studying the books she'd had shipped to her.

"Why bother?" one of the snobbier guests asked when comparing the Thoroughbred to the blacks she had purchased from Carmen. He gestured disparagingly at the Hanoverians that looked nothing like the blacks but would, she hoped, produce a fantastic draft horse that even she with her pampered horses could see was necessary here in Australia.

"Not everyone has a need for my babies," she crooned as she patted one of her spoiled and coddled Thoroughbreds who affectionately nibbled at the sleeve of her cape. She smiled at the horse, knowing each and every one of the horses born since she had imported them and those she'd sent for from her English stud. She looked at the snob and continued, "And not everyone can afford them either. I would hate to see one of these," she said, patting the Thoroughbred's rump as she sent him off with one of the grooms, "hooked up to a wagon. But one of these," she stated, petting the nose on one of the few black mares that she owned, "and their offspring will make fine draft horses, and they are still good for riding." She petted the mare again, earning an affectionate rub as the mare also attempted to combat the incessant flies. Alinta had given her a recipe and shown her the plants to combat the bugs from the Outback. It was different here near the mountains, where the cold kept some of the bugs away, or perhaps they were worse in the Outback. They applied the recipe regularly, but with everything going on this week, perhaps someone had forgotten. "And, they aren't bad to look at," she understated, knowing how beautiful the black horses were. Some of her guards were around the barns and paddocks,

dressed as stockmen because although the Thoroughbreds were valuable, the blacks too were expensive and desirable.

"Well, I could see one of these ahead of my buggy," he acceded, "but those—I just don't understand your reasoning," he said, nodding to the Hanoverian.

"We all need to experiment to get the best horses for the job," she said kindly, getting annoyed finally by him but smiling sweetly. She had the room, the time, and the money to attempt to breed some really fine horses. Not just the beautiful Thoroughbreds she loved and adored. She'd sent a couple out to Mel who had specifically requested them, and Mel had written about breeding them to Diablo, her black stud. Abigail wished she could see the offspring that had resulted, especially after Mel gushed over the beauties she assured her had resulted of the pairing. Her own mares from Carmen had given her beautiful foals but nothing outstanding. The black gene was strong and paramount in the offspring, but she wished she had a stallion to breed to some of her Thoroughbred mares to see more of a variety. She was pleased with her results so far. The Hanoverian and black cross—whatever Carmen had used to get her consistently beautiful horses—was going to be interesting to watch as the few foals she had grew up.

It was on one of the last days of her weeklong party that she took a group into one of the high meadows along the mountains she had fallen in love with. When they stopped to give the horses a breather, a gunshot rang out and everyone looked around to find out where it came

from. But when the countess tumbled from her mount, pandemonium broke out.

About the Author

K'Anne Meinel is the BEST-SELLING author of LAWYERED, REPRESENTED, SAPPHIC SURFER, DOCTORED, VEIL OF SILENCE, SURVIVORS, VETTED and CAVALCADE as well as several other books including her first, SHIPS which was written in 2003 over the course of two weeks. A gypsy at heart, she has lived in many locations and plans to continue roaming. Videos of several of her books are available on YouTube outlining some of the locations of her books and telling a little bit more…giving the readers insight into her mind as she created these wonderful stories.

K'Anne Meinel is a prolific Lesbian-Fiction bestselling and multi-award-winning author with more than 130 published works including shorts, novellas, and novels in English. Most of her work has been translated and now there are several hundred in Spanish, Portuguese, French, Italian, German, and even Japanese.

She writes in Romance, Drama, Fiction, Murder, Mystery and several other genres and is an American author born in Milwaukee, Wisconsin and raised outside Oconomowoc. Upon early graduation from high school, she went to a private college in Milwaukee and then moved to California for seventeen years before returning to Wisconsin for a couple of decades. Then, hitting the road, her adventures fuel her writings.

She is known for her wonderful, realistic, and detailed backgrounds, her stories make you feel like you are 'there,' as a part of the story yourself. Named the lesbian Danielle Steel of her time, K'Anne continues to write interesting stories in a variety of genres in both the lesbian and mainstream fiction categories.
You can learn more @ www.kannemeinel.com.

Follow along … you never know what K'Anne might come up with next!

If you have enjoyed **OUTBACK LADY**, I hope you will enjoy this excerpt from

PIRATED HEART

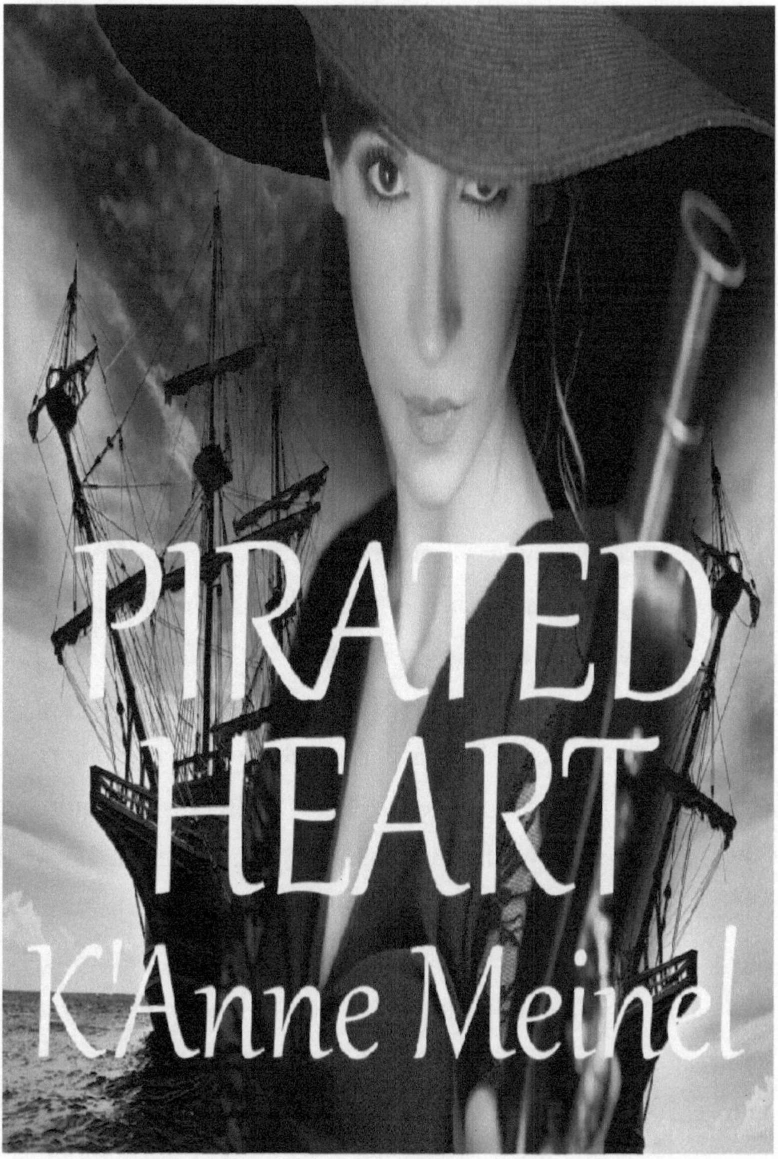

PIRATED HEART
K'Anne Meinel

~A swashbuckling good time~

From China to India to Africa and home to England...Will the love that Bettina Carmichaels shares with her wife, Claire, stand the test of time? Will it even last the second year of marriage?

Trading, pirating, sword fights, sea battles, near drownings, and imprisonment...a sailor's life may not be for all. Come along as Tina, also known as 'Black Betty,' and Claire attempt to repair their failing marriage and survive sailing on the high seas...

CHAPTER ONE

As she made her way through the busy streets, Tina couldn't remember being this angry before. She didn't bother with hiring a rickshaw, instead, preferring to push people out of her way, taking her frustrations out on anyone who dared to try and bump her.

What had Claire been thinking? To get engaged *to a man*? *That* man? *Any* man? She was married to Tina! While it wasn't quite *legal*, they had stood before God and man, and pledged themselves to each other! Claire was *her* wife!

The walk back to the port calmed her anger. She realized she would have to calm down to think rationally. Her first thoughts of gathering her exhausted crew and storming the house, turning that party into a scene of chaos, would not help things. She had to think this out. She was so angry she almost kicked a ball of fur out of her way, her boot stopping mid kick when she realized at the last moment it was a kitten. Feeling low for taking her anger out on the helpless animal, she scooped it up instead and petted it as she strode along. It was a healing balm as she stroked its soft coat.

"Captain?" a voice questioned at her elbow and she turned with a start, not realizing she had been approached until it was almost too late. This kind of absentmindedness could get her killed if she wasn't careful.

"What do you want?" she asked in a crabby-sounding voice. She stroked the kitten to help keep her calm. She wanted to take out her sword and run someone through!

"It's that Chinaman," the voice of one of her men said in an almost quavering voice. He could see the signs of ire on his captain's face and he'd seen her in a fury one too many times.

"Which one?" she asked as she gestured all about them. The streets were packed with Chinamen and women. They were, after all, in China.

"The one with the pots?" he reminded her.

Tina sighed, but not aloud. Breathing through her nose to settle her anger over Claire's defection, she realized that killing someone, perhaps one of her own men, wouldn't solve anything. She petted the kitten a little more, noticing the perfect brown tips on the ends of its much lighter base fur. It was a pretty combination. Each paw was like a brown sock. "You mean the one with the porcelain?" she asked for clarification.

"Yes, sir…ma'am…uh, Captain," he stuttered. Her anger was a palpable thing. He was surprised that the kitten she was petting hadn't been strangled. Instead, they could both hear its purring despite the noise of humanity in the throngs around them.

"What about him?"

"He says since yer a woman, he's gotta meet ya," he answered worriedly. He knew he wasn't much of a trader, but he'd visited the man first thing upon their return, knowing the profits from the porcelain they purchased would please the captain.

Tina sighed aloud. It wasn't the first time the novelty of dealing with a female captain had intrigued someone. She nodded curtly and headed on down the street, the sailor, a former pirate, following in her wake. Her long strides, when she was able to use them in the mass of humanity around them, enabled her to move quickly. Once back at the rowboat, where another of her crew was minding it, she got in without a word. As the sailor got in to row her back to their ship, they were hailed.

"Captain?!" a familiar voice called.

Tina turned sharply. She recognized that voice, but she had thought she would never hear it again. He was dead, wasn't he? She stood up as she also recognized the man striding rapidly along the dock.

"James!" she called incredulously, putting down the kitten as she pulled herself back up on the dock. "I thought you were dead."

He grabbed her in a manly hug, pulled back, and then clasped both her arms at the elbow. "Oh, I thought I was too," he confided with an infectious grin. "Fortunately, Davey Jones didn't want me."

"What in the hell happened to you?" she said in a voice that betrayed her pent-up emotions. She was thrilled to see his familiar face.

"Damn storm knocked me off my feet," he answered as he let her go. He glanced down at the two sailors listening avidly and nodded to them both, exchanging smiles of welcome. "Somehow I managed to stay afloat despite those huge waves. Then something hit me in the head and I grabbed on. It was a barrel and I managed to hold on for a while. When I felt my strength going, I found a board wide enough for me body and latched on. I tell you, I was exhausted from the battering I got. More than once I threw up more sea water than my body could handle. It was days, but somehow I found myself alive and in the middle of nowhere. I still wasn't safe, I tell ya." He wiped his brow from the heat before he continued for his captive audience. "I don't know how long I floated before I spotted a ship. They did not speak no English, but we made out. I was more concerned about slavers," he confided. "Somehow I got back here, and when I saw the Black…" he quickly corrected himself from revealing the true name of their boat, "er, the Red Bettina come into the harbor, I was thrilled. Been trying to catch up to you. Didn't expect to see you come back without Lady Claire." He looked beyond her at the small rowboat as though she had hidden her wife there.

At the mention of her wife, Tina lost the smile she had been sporting at James' return. He noted it and asked, "What happened to Lady Claire?"

"She's engaged to be married. I crashed her engagement party!"

"She's *what?!*" He was aghast at the news. Everyone knew how in love the captain was with her wife, and her wife with this red-headed beauty.

She nodded to confirm he had heard right.

"Shall I gather the men and we…" he began, outraged at the news.

She shook her head, saddened and angry, knowing to act rashly might be a bad thing. They were, after all, in a foreign port. She didn't know the man her wife was *engaged* to or the power he might wield. "I've got some business to attend to. Could you see to the repairs on the ship while I do some trading?"

He was puzzled; sure she would want to storm the house and gather her wife. He nodded at her request.

"Let's go. I need to change and pack for a few days."

James went to get in the rowboat and Tina cautioned him, "Careful of me new cat."

"You need a cat?" he asked, amused, as he saw the small, bedraggled kitten.

"Oh damn," she exclaimed, remembering that Sir Barkley had been left up at the house.

"Something else wrong, Captain?"

Tina climbed back in the rowboat and her men shoved off, pulling strongly to get them around and through the many boats in the harbor. "I left Sir Barkley at the house. He wasn't there when I saw the party and…" she left off, unsure what to do at the moment.

"We'll get him," he promised.

"Damn right we will. And me wife," she replied with a show of anger.

Tina changed in record time. She looked around her apartment on the ship as she packed a few things to be away for a time. The apartment hadn't been cleaned since the typhoon. She had been too busy to clean it before and now she was too depressed. The fine furnishings were either broken or lying about, waiting to be straightened up. Her clothes were scattered and she swore under her breath as she looked for certain outfits to pack. Finally, she was ready. It was pitch black out, but the best time for her to leave the ship if anyone was watching.

The crew, the ones left on ship, had greeted James effusively. She gave him a few last-minute commands about the repairs on the ship and asked him to take care of her new cat. Calling to Frank, who was to accompany her, and Leonard, the crewman who knew the porcelain dealer, they got back into the rowboat to leave.

"I arranged transportation," Leonard told her as he rowed for the far shore of the Pearl River Delta.

"Where are we going, exactly?" she asked, wondering. She trusted her men, but she wanted to be prepared. She had her knife at her waist, another in her boot, as well as her sword, but wondered if she should have strapped on her scimitars as well.

"He lives up over those hills," he pointed with his chin at the hills surrounding the harbor. Even though it was night, their shadows were darker than the night itself. The harbor was still busy despite the lateness of the hour.

"He wants us to come to his home?"

"Aye," he answered, short and sweet. He wasn't a verbose man, but trying to get the best deal on the goods they had been trading for, he had learned when to stay quiet and when to speak up.

"What else does he trade in?" she asked, to keep her mind off her personal life and concentrate on the trade. After all, that was why they were in China.

After a long and boring recitation about fragrant woods and exotic incense as well other trade goods, he had rowed them across what would someday be called Victoria Harbor. The Kowloon Peninsula, which was the mainland from the islands in the harbor, was their destination on the far side of the Pearl River.

"There is an inn we can stay at," Leonard stated as they pulled up and tied off the rowboat. They all wondered if it would still be here when they needed it to go back to the ship. "They have horses for rent and I'd asked them for four since I didn't know if Lady…" he left off as he realized that Lady Claire was a sore subject for the captain at this moment.

Tina didn't say a word, still concentrating on the trade. She tried not to think too much about her wife. "Let's go. I'm tired," she admitted as they headed away from the harbor for the inn that Leonard recommended. She would spend a sleepless night tossing and turning.

CHAPTER TWO

Tina's ass was sore. Not having ridden a horse in quite a while, she was unused to using those muscles in quite that way. Still, despite the fatigue, she was able to meet their host. The trip had taken up almost the whole day as they rode over the deceptively distant hills and into a valley where their host lived.

Meeting Liú Zhāng was very interesting. He was a man of great height in a land she had found normally had shorter people. He was an impressive sight as he stood there on his steps to greet her personally. His home was extensive, with the telltale overhanging roof of red tile and the typical Chinese architecture.

Tina got off her horse and stood for a moment, steadying her tired and saddlesore body before she turned to hand her reigns to one of her host's servants. Looking about, she saw the walls of her host's home were high and guarded. "How did you meet this guy?" she hissed at Leonard, but didn't expect a reply as they began to climb the steps.

Liú Zhāng looked at the woman, dressed as a man, walking up his steps. If not for the telltale bumps on her chest, he would have thought her a man…a very striking-looking man. She took strides like a man. She dressed as he had seen sailors from all over the world. Her knife and her sword looked well-used. Her red hair was intriguing. She definitely had European features in smooth, white skin. She was dark from captaining a ship, the winds whipping at her skin, but she also looked very healthy, very physically fit. The European women he had seen in the city were mostly gone to fat from too much good living.

"Mr. Liú Zhāng, may I present me captain, Captain Carmichaels," Leonard said formally.

Tina bowed a little, but didn't take her eyes off their host. She had seen him assessing her as she approached. She also recognized the look in his eye; it was definitely attraction. She had assessed him as well and found him comely. He was larger than the average Chinaman she had met. He was definitely a warrior within that great body of a man, standing ramrod straight. She wondered if he had been in the military.

Another man approached rapidly and, speaking to their host, he interpreted for them. Liú replied in rapid Chinese and bowed to Tina as their interpreter said, "His greatness, Master Liú Zhāng, greets you."

Liú also said something else, which the interpreter repeated, "His greatness would welcome you into his home." With a gesture of sweeping her into the house through the large wooden doors, it was a clear indication that Tina should go first.

Tina wasn't sure she liked the idea of giving her back to anyone, but he had invited her here to meet with her for trade. She had to trust at some point and hope she wouldn't have to pull her knife or her sword.

The home was large and airy with screens that could be pulled aside for privacy. Low-seated cushions everywhere gave the illusion of couches. Women shuffled around in the odd walk that Tina had seen in the upper crust of the Chinese. These women were not like the ones down in the harbor who hawked their wares or sold their bodies; the women here were refined and delicate. Like the porcelain her host made, their skin was white and soft and very clean. These women were well taken care of. They did not make eye contact as Tina and her men were seated along with their host and interpreter. They did bring tea, which Tina detested, but which she sipped delicately from the fine porcelain cups it was served in. Her interest in the cups themselves was apparent.

Their host wasted no time asking about her through the interpreter, "How long have you been a captain?"

"Many years. My grandfather was a sea captain and he taught me. He brought me to China several years ago and I've always wanted to return."

"Is it common for Europeans to have female captains?"

She laughed and shook her head. Her hair had grown considerably since she cut it so long ago, and during her journey that day it had come loose. The curls that cascaded down her back shook with her head, fascinating their host. "I think I am rather unique to that."

He enjoyed their conversation as she was frank with him, and, he felt, honest. It was refreshing. So many foreigners came to China and tried to cheat them in trade. He felt she was different. Not just because she was a woman, but because she was a captain and knew her trade goods. He was very intrigued. He felt himself attracted as well. They talked long into the afternoon, eventually taking a walk around the grounds accompanied by her men and the interpreter.

Tina watched as he showed her the gardens and his home. It was apparent, he took pride in it. It was beautiful, almost a paradise. It was well-guarded as well. She saw the men on the walls surrounding the home estate. He explained he owned several villages where his porcelain was made for him to trade. He got good trades to feed them all and clothe them. He was also a farmer.

By the evening meal, as they continued to talk, Tina could tell that Frank and Leonard were getting antsy. She found the conversation with Liú Zhāng to be very fascinating and it had held her interest all afternoon. She had barely thought about her life and her wife. She'd done enough thinking on that subject on the ride up here with plenty of time for introspection.

Liú had noticed his guest's lapses in conversation, the expression in her amazing green eyes turning sorrowful from time to time. He wondered at it. He also noticed the two men who had accompanied her had lost interest in their varied conversation. Apparently, talking about gardens and growing vegetables was not their interest.

"Your grandfather must send me these woods you tell me," the interpreter, who they had learned was called, Féng, told them.

"Your woods are just as intriguing to us," she said as she ate the interesting food that his wives had served them. She was intrigued that he had no qualms about stating that he had five wives and a couple of concubines.

"I don't have as many wives as the emperor Jiajing," he laughed as they continued their cordial conversation long into the night.

Tina had given up the thought of sleeping long ago. Both of her men, after the long walk about the grounds and good food, had fallen asleep on the many cushions that made up the floor couches, as she thought of them. Their snores and farts could be heard as she and their host talked over and around them. She was too fascinated to sleep. This man was a living, breathing, bit of history. He shared China in a way that few, if any men, could. She wondered at how advanced he was for a man of China, how liberal to be treating her as a valued guest instead of a mere woman.

"Our great leader and his naval forces repulsed the Portuguese at Tuen Mun," he told her. She already knew of the great battles of 1521 and 1522, but hearing him brag of their own side of history was interesting.

When he went on to tell her of the 1542 invasion by Altan Khan, she leaned forward to listen. She could hardly wait for Féng to interpret. His misunderstanding of some English words was amusing and annoying by turns. Altan Khan had even reached the outskirts of Beijing in 1550. General Qui Jiguang, a distant relative of her host—which explained his own military bearing as well as his affluence—was instrumental in the defeat of Altan Khan.

"You must be careful of the wokou pirates," he explained. They had been attacking the southeastern coastline and the general had been sent to stop them.

Hearing of pirate attacks in this part of the world, Tina got an almost nostalgic look in her eye for the enjoyment of old. Being a trader was clearly not as fun or exciting; however, it was respectable.

Féng was exhausted and his voice was becoming hoarse from the long hours his master had made him translate. His head ached from trying to keep the words in both languages straight, but he would not fail his master since the beating that would ensue would be terrible. He too could tell of the attraction his master felt for this woman and was not surprised when he offered to share her bed.

"I thank your master for the invitation," Tina replied carefully, "but I must respectfully decline."

"Do the morals of European women forbid the sharing of bodies?" she was asked.

She nodded. "European women cleave only to their spouses."

"Is the captain married?"

She nodded again and Liú noticed the sadness had returned to those green eyes. "Yes, I am."

"Your husband, he does not mind your manly pursuits?"

She shook her head. "I have no husband." As she saw the look in his eye telling her she was confusing him, she explained, "I have the cut sleeve."

As the interpreter explained to his master, she saw the look in Liú's own black eyes turn from one of confusion to one of understanding. He nodded as he asked for clarification of her term. "Pleasures of the bitten peach," was the terminology he used and that referred to homosexuality. Her cut sleeve was an acronym of the phrase.

"Europeans accept this?" she was asked.

She shook her head. "No," was all she replied.

"Here, it is not well known. I, however, have traveled," he explained. "I have seen more. I understand more than those who have never left their villages."

Tina understood more than he was saying. Having traveled herself and seen so many interesting sights around the world, she was more accepting. Were she not married to Claire, she would have taken him up on his offer. He was a fascinating and cosmopolitan man. That he would talk to her for these many hours on a variety of subjects, showed her that. She would have enjoyed sharing his body. She had male lovers in her past, but she still considered herself married to Claire. She would take care of that in due time. Right now, it was very late. She had had a long day and needed her sleep. Her host had her shown to a private bedroom.

The servants who attended her showed no signs they had been roused from their own sleep at this ungodly hour. They took her to the women's baths and she was given a robe. She was made to understand her clothes would be laundered while she slept. The women had been amused that she wouldn't give up her knives or sword and slept with them near at hand.

Liú considered keeping the female captain. She was attractive, a warrior woman, and would breed up fine sons. But he also recognized that she would fight him to the end and possibly kill him. He didn't doubt that the weapons she openly carried were well-used by the woman. He was disappointed that she wouldn't share herself with him, but he found, to his surprise, that he respected her, almost as much as he would a man. She was obviously well-educated, something he had never found in a woman before. He regretfully decided to trade with her, but he hoped to remain something he had never contemplated with a woman before—a friend.

Over the next couple of days, Tina was privileged to see her host, Lord Liú Zhāng's, small porcelain works. He explained it wasn't as large as the emperor's porcelain works in Jingdezhen as they didn't have the same amounts of clay available to them. His small factories created porcelain as fine as the emperor's, but because they weren't official porcelain manufactories, they went unnoticed and he was able to sell their creations outside the country.

White clay was mined from the local mountain in small quantities. Water-powered pestles crushed the rock into a fine powder. The powder was then mixed with water, cleaned of impurities, and formed into bricks. These were allowed to dry, crushed again, and then the remaining impurities leeched out of the clay until they had the final white clay they mixed to a consistency that allowed their artisans to begin to form the cups, bowls, vases, and other creations that were so breathtaking and fine.

Watching the water power harnessed from local streams, Tina was impressed with the innovations these people were using. It saved a lot of muscle work to have the mechanisms pound out the clay until it was fine powder. She also saw how it turned the lathes to form the various pieces that she hoped to purchase.

"Why is he giving us the grand tour, I'd like to know?" muttered Leonard darkly. He was tired, he was bored, and he was regretting pursuing this line of trade for the captain. Still, Tina seemed very interested in the process.

"Why are you showing me this? I may steal your secrets and set up my own shop," Tina teased her host.

Liú was amused at his guest's playful banter with him. Few, if any, dared. He was a most imposing figure. "Good luck with that," his interpreter warned her.

Tina laughed. She was enjoying herself. It was fascinating watching them work. They had stopped until Liú commanded his workers back to work.

"We do not have the clay that the emperor's factories have; however, our small works make impressive art," he bragged, showing off their work. The heat from the kilns made it too hot to get very close to that part of the manufactory. Men were constantly bringing in wood to fire them and keep the heat consistent. Prayers were offered to the kiln god to keep the heat steady, but the man in charge, who watched for the blue white flames, could judge and kept them going.

"Have you ever done this work?" she asked, her British accent very apparent in her question.

His own interpreter had noted the variations in the English captain's voice. One question might be purely British and at other times, her English was not quite so…cultivated. Liú nodded before he told her, "I was much more suited to fight rather than make bowls with these." He held out his hands, showing the callused palms.

"Ah, but I'm sure your workers," she gestured at the artisans, "make fine porcelain with just as callused hands," she teased.

He laughed as the translation came through. He had to concede her point. He was just not suited for this work and he made that clear.

"What are they doing?" she asked, alarmed, as they were shown where someone was taking great pride in breaking some of the pieces.

"Those pieces do not pass inspection," she was told.

"But they are so beautiful," she contradicted, looking at the large pile of porcelain chards.

"Beautiful, yes. Flawed, yes. We will not trade those that do not pass."

She could see no flaw in the pieces that were destroyed, but the remaining ones, those she hoped to trade for, were absolutely breathtaking.

Later, after a light lunch, he showed off his battle skills, hoping to glean the pretty captain's favor by showing her how well he handled the sword. Although he knew they would never sleep together and he regretted that, he also wanted to impress the white European woman. She impressed him greatly.

Tina was captivated. Not only by the skills of his workers, but by the man himself. Seeing him stripped to the waist and battling not one, but two of his soldiers, he showed innate skill. Even with a pole he battled until he was dripping sweat.

Tina surprised her host by indicating she wished to do battle with him. At first, he refused. A woman fighting a man was most…unnatural. However, after much debate through Féng, he finally acquiesced. He was intrigued that she chose to use her own sword. The Chinese swords were thinner, sharper, and much more elegant than the sturdy sword she used.

Once he agreed, she immediately went on the offensive, attacking viciously. Liú found himself nearly losing to the mad woman she had become. Fighting back, he held himself in check from hurting her, and Tina, with a gleam in her eye to show she knew what he was doing, continued to take advantage of him. Realizing she wasn't about to let him win, that she had skills of her own, he fought back in earnest, Tina rose to the challenge.

The men who had fought their master watched in awe as the captain, a woman captain at that, and an inferior European, fought and was nearly besting him. Only his taller body, more muscular than the woman's, began to wear on her.

Tina, who had thought to have the advantage because Liú was fatigued after showing off with his men, found herself on the defensive. Her speed and agility made up for the muscles that were rippling through him. Much to his surprise, it had him nearly dropping and conceding more than once. Had they actually been striking each other, to play to the death and going for blood, both would have been in trouble at this point. By using their swords off each other, their muscles were taking the brunt of the blows.

Liú thought he finally had her when Tina, exhausted from their long combat, fell to her knees. His blow would have been fatal, but as he lowered his own sword hers had come up and would have emasculated him. He burst out laughing as Féng interpreted for him, telling her he would concede to a draw. Tina looked up at him with her own mirth deep in her eyes. He held out his hand to help her up.

"Well played," Féng interpreted for Liú.

Tina fully enjoyed the women's baths that afternoon. Her muscles were very sore from fighting with Liú, but she had enjoyed herself immensely. It had allowed her to take out other frustrations on the fight. Little did she know she was being watched by the lusty man through a peep hole.

Liú was not surprised to see that the European woman had a muscular body, which had been well-hidden under those manly clothes she wore. What surprised him was the length of the red hair she wore clubbed back. As he viewed her physically fit body he was amazed to see that there was no body hair, not under her arms, not on her mons, not on her legs. Did European women not grow hair in those places? He would have to find out at some point. He regretted that he couldn't find out from this incredible specimen.

As Tina and her men prepared to leave the next day, she was pleased that Liú and a few of his men had decided to accompany them back to the harbor. They had worked out the pieces he would allow her to buy from him and his people were already gathering them, cushioning and covering them in straw, and placing them in barrels. The carts would leave as soon as they were ready and packed. He had been most generous.

"My men," he indicated his soldiers and the interpreter Féng, "will help escort my people back with the valuable trade goods." He and Tina both knew it was an excuse, but neither said anything more about it.

Liú made the ride back seem short as he explained the rich history of porcelain. From the famed city of Jingdezhen in the Jiangxi province, they made porcelain for the emperor and his many homes. They had made pottery for hundreds of years.

"The cobalt is painted on the vessels and then, when fired, it turns that rich blue," it was explained. "Limestone and more clay stone are mixed to glaze the pieces," he further went on. "Smaller pieces are dipped in the solution. My people spray the larger pieces with a tube from their mouths directly onto the pieces. Red is made from copper." Tina was fascinated, not only by his knowledge, but by his pride in the product his people, whom he owned, created for them. He in turn sold it to provide them all with food, trade goods, and other necessities. Tina never mentioned how she felt about slave labor, but she found that he took good care of his people.

Tina in turn told him of England, Canada, and other places she had traveled, intriguing him with her knowledge and travel. He himself had been to the Great Wall, which even now was being finished to protect China from the Mongols who tried to invade their vast country.

As they neared the city, Tina was surprised to hear a noise that was familiar to her, so familiar in fact, that at first she dismissed it as entirely coincidental. She finally looked up as it was repeated, frantically, and realized that Sir Barkley was the one making the noise and it was his bark that had alerted her to his presence. The sound was not at the house she had rented for herself, Claire, and the other captains in her fleet, but at a totally strange and unfamiliar house. She stopped her horse so abruptly that the others went on a few paces before realizing she wasn't with them.

"What the hell?" Frank asked, realizing what had stopped his captain.

"It's Sir Barkley!" She looked for him. "You hear him too, do you not, Frank?" she asked for verification, thinking she was going mad. She spotted the familiar black and white mass of doghood on a balcony of a house surrounded with walls. How the dog had spotted her, she did not know, but he was reared up on the balcony and someone was trying unsuccessfully to pull the large Newfoundland dog down from his perch. He was determined and as stubborn as his human. He was barking his head off to get her attention. Seeing her stop and look for him, he wagged his tail madly, the tone of his barks changing from frantic to welcoming.

"What is going on?" Liú had turned his horse back and Féng interpreted for him.

"My dog is in that house," Tina replied as she got off her horse, handed the reigns to Leonard, and walked determinedly up to the gate of the house.

The gatekeeper would not let her pass, nor would he even try to understand her attempts to speak to him. He plainly ignored the madwoman. It was not until Féng interpreted for the wild-haired female that he even deigned to notice. It was when he spotted Liú Zhāng that his demeanor turned to one of obedience and subservience. He allowed them in the courtyard, where they were met by a very imposing man.

"What do you want here?" he asked them and Féng, upon orders from Liú, interpreted for the English people.

"That is my dog. How did he wind up here?" Tina asked.

The man looked down his nose at the impertinent female asking him questions through an interpreter. Only the recognized presence of Liú Zhāng kept him from ignoring her and throwing her out of his home. "I traded for that dog and he is mine," he insisted, his tone one of belligerence. Even without the translation, the words sounded clipped and angry.

"How much would you trade for him?" Tina asked.

"He is not for sale. I am assured he is one of a kind."

Knowing exactly how one of a kind he was, she wasn't sure how to proceed to get her dog returned to her. "Who sold him to you? A woman?" she asked, feeling her heart sinking at the thought that Claire would betray her in this way too.

"No mere woman would own such a magnificent beast as this," he sneered. The translation of the words made Tina smolder.

"But I assure you, the dog knows me and is mine," she insisted. Sir Barkley had kept up a constant barrage of barks despite the two servants attempting to silence him and pull him from his perch.

In rapid Chinese, the man called to his servants. One of them attempted to grab Sir Barkley around the muzzle, but the dog easily pulled away and continued to bark. A hand was raised and Tina went for her sword.

Liú Zhāng had watched as Tina attempted to reason with the man. He knew the man would not give up the dog. He also knew something Tina did not. The man would probably breed the dog to another large dog and their puppies would make him a fortune, not in the beast itself, but in their fur. The man was a fur trader. The dog's value was in its pelt. He could see it was a solid, monstrous beast, well-built, and obviously trying to get to the woman. When he saw Tina go for her sword, he stopped her hand.

"No, this is not the way to handle this," he had Féng interpret for him.

"Can't you just order him or something…" she asked before she could really think.

"I cannot," he returned stiffly, rising straight and proud with his military bearing.

Tina acknowledged that she had gone too far, but Sir Barkley was her dog. There had to be a way. "You won't sell or trade the dog?" she asked again, hoping the man would be reasonable.

"I think it is time that you and your party leave," the man said, but not to the mere woman, to Liú.

Liú nodded. The man had rights. Tina did not. She was a foreigner and a woman. He could not intervene. The dog was lost to her. He explained as best he could, but he could sense her fury. It was very…arousing.

"I will be back," Tina warned through Féng.

The man ignored her and turned away to return to his home.

Sir Barkley would not stop barking. Tina called to him, "Quiet!" He immediately halted his noise, wagging his tail to show he understood and there were no hard feelings. "Stay," she further called. She hoped he wouldn't think she was abandoning him. She took care to memorize where this home was in relation to her own rental in the city. She was alarmed to realize their path took them right by it. She wondered what Claire was doing at this moment as they made their way down to the harbor. They had come a different way from their original path to Liú Zhāng's home. Once they arrived at the harbor in the company of he and his men, she sent Leonard back with their rented horses to retrieve their rowboat. She signaled the ship to send another for her and Frank. She would arrange for the trade goods to be exchanged immediately.

"Well, this is goodbye," Tina said sadly as they waited for the boat.

"I hope you will write. I have enjoyed our visit," Liú said honestly. He wondered that he had never felt like this with another woman. Even with his first wife, he was unable to talk as he had with this European woman.

"I will write. I too have enjoyed this visit and learned so much."

As she watched him ride away she was pleased to see him look back. Féng had looked relieved to end his duties as interpreter.

"That was an interestin' visit," Frank said cautiously. The captain of old had returned and her interest in that Zhāng chap was apparent. He hadn't seen that since Claire had come into the captain's life.

"Fascinating," Tina agreed as the rowboat arrived for them.

TO BE CONTINUED…

~End sample chapter of PIRATED HEART~
For more go check out all my books at: www.kannemeinel.com to purchase the complete book or for many other delightful offerings

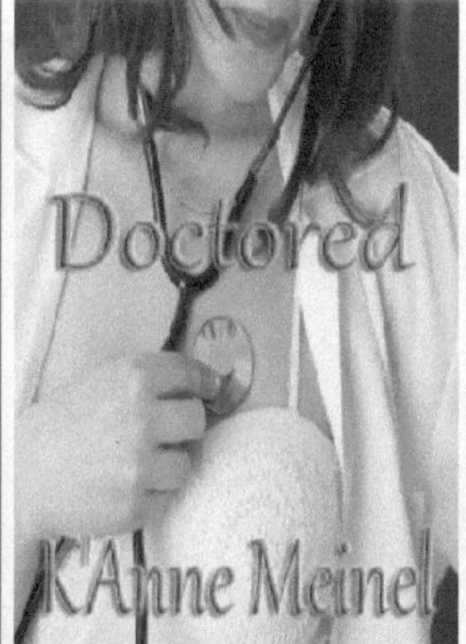

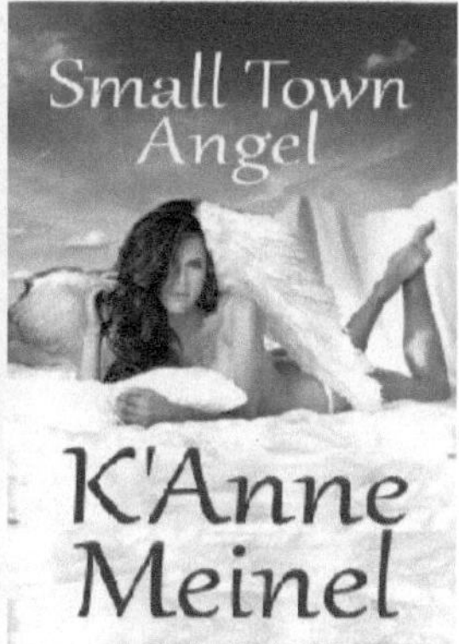

www.kannemeinel.com

Shadoe
Publishing

www.ingramcontent.com/pod-product-compliance
Lightning Source LLC
LaVergne TN
LVHW091136080826
845145LV00008B/2174